He stroked her.

"You feel so good," he said. He trailed his fingers down her cheek as he stood above her, shirt open and shirttails loose.

Alana couldn't meet his piercing gaze. Yet looking straight ahead proved equally hazardous. She viewed the dark blond hair curling down the center of his chest to his navel, to his low-slung jeans. His chest looked good, hard and strong. Staring at the simple brass belt buckle above his fly sent a sudden, unwanted surge of arousal through her.

As if he could read her mind, Judd brought her hand to his lips and pressed a kiss to her palm.

She heard herslf moan. *This shouldn't be happening. We shouldn't start something we can't finish. We shouldn't—*

And then he was weaving his fingers into her dark, wet hair, angling her face to his, touching his mouth to hers.

She moaned again, unable to stop him. Unable to stop herself.

Dear Reader,

Hanukkah has come to mean different things to different people. In America, where Christmas is such an all-encompassing event, Hanukkah offers Jews a way to join in the merriment of the season. It's an opportunity to cook special foods, to revive old traditions, to fill our homes with the bright warmth of burning candles during the darkest, coldest nights of the year.

It's also an opportunity to contemplate the meaning of freedom.

The holiday celebrates the military victory of the Jews over the Syrians in 164 B.C. During the Syrian occupation of Jerusalem, many Jews were killed, others went into hiding, and those who remained in the city were forced to abandon their own customs and traditions and adopt the habits of the Syrians. Once the Jews regained their city and reconsecrated their temple, they were able to stop pretending to be something they weren't. They won back not only their city and their temple, but their identity.

To me, this is Hanukkah's essential message: We all deserve the freedom to define ourselves, to discover truth and faith in our own ways.

My husband and I are a "mixed" marriage, so we celebrate both Hanukkah and Christmas. We honor the rituals of our ancestors and create new rituals of our own. In our living room we display a decorated fir tree, and in our kitchen we display the silver menorah that once belonged to my grandmother. Our sons are equally familiar with the eight candles and the eight reindeer. They are proud of their double heritage, and we consider them—and ourselves—doubly blessed.

I wish you and your loved ones the best of the season, however you celebrate it. Happy Hanukkah! Merry Christmas! Joyous Kwanzaa! Festive Solstice! Peace and goodwill—and freedom—to all.

Judith

JUDITH ARNOLD
SWEET LIGHT

Harlequin Books

TORONTO • NEW YORK • LONDON
AMSTERDAM • PARIS • SYDNEY • HAMBURG
STOCKHOLM • ATHENS • TOKYO • MILAN
MADRID • WARSAW • BUDAPEST • AUCKLAND

Published December 1992

ISBN 0-373-16467-X

SWEET LIGHT

Chapter One

Alana Halpern taxied the twin-engine Beechcraft to the squat gray terminal, shut down the engines, and took a deep breath. The next two hours were critical.

Mark Neeley had told her as much when he'd roused her from a deep sleep at six o'clock that morning. "Alana, sweetheart," he'd said in an ominously chipper voice, "I've got to ask a big favor of you."

"No." Pulling her blanket over her head, she'd extended her arm toward the night table and groped for the telephone base, anxious to hang up before she came fully awake.

Mark's voice reached her through the blanket: "Don't you dare hang up on me, Halpern! Your job is at stake!"

Groaning, she shoved the blanket out of her way and brought the receiver back to her ear. "What?" she growled.

"Are you up?"

"No."

"I need you to fly to New Hampshire for me. We've got a potential client stranded up there. His name is Judd Singer, and we want his account, Alana."

Maybe Mark Neeley wanted Judd Singer's account. Maybe his partners at Neeley, Henderson wanted it. Maybe all the hotshot hustle-bustle account executives wanted it.

All Alana wanted was eight hours of uninterrupted sleep.

She sighed. "Flying to New Hampshire to pick up your stranded potential clients is not my job, Mark. I'm a graphic artist, not a pilot."

"You've got a pilot's license."

"So do the flight crews of most major airlines. Can't this guy catch a puddle jumper out of Laconia?"

"Alana," Mark said unctuously. "Of course he could. But is that the way to get our hands on his account? We want to go the extra mile for him. We're talking about Judd Singer, the founder and owner of the Magic Shops."

"*You're* talking about him."

"We're talking about an up-and-coming entrepreneur with an expanding chain of high-class toy stores. He's about to go big time and he's shopping for an advertising agency. It would be a fantastic opportunity for Neeley, Henderson. We've just got to show him how much we care, and I think sending a private plane up there to get him and bring him back to Boston to meet with us all would make a big impression on him."

"Fine. Send a private plane. Rent a pilot."

"Why rent a pilot when we've got you?"

Her yawn effectively garbled the expletive that filled her mouth. She never should have let anyone at the agency know she had her pilot's license. At first, it was nothing more than a novelty—like Bill McCloy's ability to walk on his hands or Tracy Rollins's fluency in Urdu—but eventually it became a significant asset.

It wasn't that she minded flying a client every now and then. But she minded it today. "Mark, tonight is the first night of Hanukkah."

"And?"

"And while that may mean nothing to you, it happens to mean something to me. My parents are throwing a party in Brookline tonight. It's my nephew Michael's first Hanukkah. This is a big deal."

"Forgive me if I'm presuming, Alana, but don't your holidays start after sundown?"

"Yes, but—"

"So, you'll fly up to New Hampshire, fly back with Mr. Singer, deliver him into my welcoming embrace by around two in the afternoon, and—I'll sweeten the deal—you can take the rest of the afternoon off. How does that sound? You can go straight to Brookline and help your mother make glopkas."

"Latkes," she corrected him. "I don't know if my mother's going to make them. Everybody's watching their cholesterol these days."

"So, you'll take the afternoon off and help your mother make steamed asparagus. How about it, Alana? Do it for me, do it for the agency, do it for a year-end bonus. Do it for Mr. Singer."

Against her better judgment, she'd done it. She'd
gotten dressed and taken a cab out to the airport in
Marlboro, where Mark had arranged to have a Beechcraft turboprop waiting for her. She'd exchanged ap-
propriately manly small talk with the maintenance
crew, cleared her flight plan, climbed into the cockpit, and by 9:00 a.m. she'd been airborne.

Two hours and fifteen minutes later, she found
herself at a minuscule airstrip outside the town of
Berlin, somewhere north of the White Mountains and
not too far south of the Canadian border. Several
inches of snow framed the cleared black tarmac and
crowned the flat roof of the terminal. The voice from
the control tower that talked her through her landing
had sounded lethargic. *Smile*, she commanded herself, shoving open the door and climbing out. *Be
charming. Win the client for Neeley, Henderson.*

As she ambled toward the terminal her breath
emerged in plumes of white; the crisp, cold air nipped
her ears. She lifted her scarf higher around her neck
and broke into a jog, eager to get inside before she
froze.

"Excuse me," she said when she reached the portly
clerk, who seemed more interested in the data flash-
ing across his computer's monitor than in her. "I've
just flown up from Massachusetts to pick up a Mr.
Judd Singer. Do you know if he's here?" She glanced
around the terminal, trying to figure out which of the
assorted folks milling about might be her passenger.

"I'll page him," the clerk said grandly. He lifted a
hand microphone and pressed the button. "Mr. Judd

Singer, please meet your party at the front counter. Judd Singer, your party is here."

No one approached. She turned back to the counter, checked her watch and pulled her flight plan from an inner pocket of her jacket. "Maybe he isn't here yet."

"I'm here," came a low, gruff voice behind her.

Alana spun around and gaped in surprise at the man sauntering toward her in long, confident strides. Her vision took in his soft, blondish brown hair, his icy blue eyes, his sharp nose and thin lips, his lined leather jacket open to reveal a plaid flannel shirt and faded blue jeans that rode low on his slim hips. On his feet were thick-soled leather work boots.

She lifted her gaze to his face again, to his harsh chin, his unsmiling mouth and his eyes, piercingly clear, set deep beneath pale eyebrows. His complexion had a golden undertone, as if in spite of the season he'd recently spent a great deal of time outdoors.

Mark had said he was a hot prospect for the agency. What he neglected to mention was that he was also rugged, tall, broad-shouldered . . . and gorgeous.

Hoping she didn't look utterly smitten, she offered him her right hand. "Alana Halpern," she said. "I'll be flying you down to the Boston area."

He gave her a slow, thorough inspection before shaking her hand. His cool blue gaze lingered for a moment on her face before inching down her athletically contoured body. She braced herself for the expected remarks about her age and her gender—men often found it impossible to believe that a twenty-eight-year-old woman could pilot a plane.

He didn't make any snide comments, however. He simply released her hand and said, "Let's go."

Not a man of many words, she thought, lowering her gaze to the battered canvas duffel bag he held in his left hand. He was supposed to be a mogul, a VIP, a power player for whose business the honchos of Neeley, Henderson were prepared to sell their souls. Yet he looked like a cross between a cowboy and a logger, with a trace of merchant marine adventurer mixed in. Shaking his hand was not like shaking the hand of an up-and-coming entrepreneur; his palm was too hard, his fingers too thick, too strong.

She was unnerved by the prospect of having to make scintillating chitchat with him all the way back to Massachusetts. For that matter, she was unnerved by the prospect of spending the next two hours sitting beside him in the small cabin of the Beechcraft, miles above the earth, surrounded by a clear December sky, all alone with the best-looking man she'd ever seen. The very idea of it sent a hot shiver down her spine.

"Okay," she said, her voice sounding steadier than her nerves. "Let's go."

SHE'S YOUNG, he thought.

Not that it bothered him. He'd had his fill of people questioning his ideas not because there was anything wrong with them but simply because he was thirty-three years old. More than questioning his ideas—a lot of people outright rejected them, ridiculed them, told him he was an arrogant kid who didn't understand the first thing about the marketplace. A lot of people thought he was some crazy fool from the boondocks who didn't quite have a grip on reality.

Hell, he knew reality better than any of them. Reality was his life. Only a brutal realist would trade in magic.

So, a girl was flying him to Boston, he pondered, following her across the tarmac to the plane. A *woman,* he corrected himself silently, although there was something mighty girlish about her thick black hair, which tumbled in waves halfway down her back. Something girlish about her round, thickly lashed eyes, which were paradoxically bright and dark at the same time, and her arching cheekbones, her lean body and coltish gait. She had long legs and trim hips. He could only imagine what lurked beneath her fleece-lined denim jacket, but given what he could see, he reckoned her proportions would be far from voluptuous.

That was okay. He preferred slender women.

Cripes, what was he thinking? She was his pilot, Mark Neeley's emissary, the ad agency's way of scoring points with a prospective client. And sure, Judd would give the agency a few points.

He studied the woman as she took her seat next to him in the tiny cockpit. He had stowed his duffel in the cargo space behind him and fastened his seat belt, and now he was free to watch her prepare for the flight. She donned a pair of sunglasses and then her headset, buckled herself in, and began conversing in official-sounding jargon with the control tower.

Judd leaned back in his seat and decided that watching her was quite all right with him. The faint aroma of gasoline mingled with other, subtler scents, *her* scents—basic soap, mint, and herbal shampoo. Her legs appeared strong yet graceful stretched out under the instrument panel, her feet poised on the rudder bar. She looked as if she knew what she was doing.

She ran through a quick check of the controls, turned on the engines and taxied toward the eastern end of the runway. He admired her fluid movements, her easy patter with the control tower, her expertise. It occurred to him that knowing how to fly a plane lent a woman a certain sex appeal.

He wondered whether she would be working on his account if he signed with Neeley, Henderson. Not that he was looking for complications, not that he was in the market for a romance, but a casual dalliance wasn't beyond imagining.

Forget it. She probably had a boyfriend, or a husband. A woman as attractive as she was didn't stay unattached for long.

She didn't address him directly until they were off the ground. "Did you have a nice stay in New Hampshire?"

He stared out the windshield. There was small talk and small talk; this qualified as microscopic. "Yeah," he answered.

"Are you planning to open one of your toy stores up here?"

Her voice was alluringly soft and smooth, her Boston accent oddly amusing. "They aren't exactly toy stores," he said laconically.

She shot him a swift, contrite look. "I'm sorry. Mark Neeley implied that they were." Her tone became brisk and mechanical as she announced her intended cruising altitude into the microphone attached to her headset. Then she returned her attention to Judd. "He said they were basically high-class toy stores."

"That's part of it."

She seemed to be waiting for him to elaborate. When he didn't, she pressed on. "What else do you sell?"

"Magic."

She gave him a slack-jawed stare.

"Equipment for magic tricks," he explained. "Also crystals, pyramids, brain puzzles."

"New Age toys," she joked. "I can see why your business is booming. People don't like to cut loose unless they can justify it with a little mysticism."

She waited for him to respond. He remained silent, though. Banter didn't come easily to him.

"It's a unique market niche," she persevered. "A good advertising campaign would capitalize on that".

He was tempted to warn her that her efforts were wasted on him. She wasn't going to win his account on the basis of this one flight, no matter how much he appreciated it. The truth was, he was less interested in her ad strategy than in the lulling texture of her voice. "What did you say your name was?"

She glanced briefly his way. "Alana Halpern."

The sun slanted blindingly against the windshield, and he envied her her sunglasses. "You work for Neeley?"

"That's right," she said, banking the plane into a curve southward and then climbing it higher, up above the dense, dark spines of the evergreens below them. "Mark Neeley's the Art Director. I do graphic design and art."

"And run their air limo service?"

She tossed him a breezy smile. "Only for their most prized clients." The plane bucked at a pocket of turbulence, then leveled itself.

He twisted in his seat so he could see her better. She had a striking profile, her nose long and straight beneath the bridge of her sunglasses, her chin cleanly delineated, her gloved hands firm on the controls. He wondered how she'd become a pilot, and why. But he refrained from asking. A private man, he respected other people's privacy, as well.

"So, what brought you to New Hampshire?" she asked.

"An artisan."

"Hmm?"

"A fellow who makes hand-crafted wooden jigsaw puzzles. I came up to have a look at his stuff."

"Was it worth the trip?"

"Yes."

The engines hummed. The sun warmed the cabin. The plane bucked over another invisible wrinkle of turbulence.

"What exactly are you looking for in an ad agency, Mr. Singer?"

Judd eyed her speculatively. He didn't want to show his hand before Neeley, Henderson—and the other agencies bidding for his business—showed theirs. "Intelligence," he finally said, revealing nothing.

Apparently, she recognized that he wasn't going to discuss his professional plans with her. "You aren't a New England native, are you?"

He gave her a slow grin. He knew she was asking just to keep the dialogue alive, yet a part of him wanted to believe she actually cared about where he came from. "Idaho," he said.

"Idaho?"

"Yes."

She turned from the controls to gawk at him again. Then she laughed. "I've never met anyone from Idaho before."

"Then I'm your first."

"You certainly are." Shaking her head, she turned forward again. "Idaho. Wow. You must think our mountains are puny."

He smiled. The mountains of New England *were* puny, but as he gazed down at the rolling contours of the terrain below, the luxuriant green of the fir trees highlighted by glimpses of granite and snatches of white snow, he appreciated the gentleness of the scenery, the forgiving nature of it. Back in Idaho, the mountains were sharp, stony and pitiless. He had spent the first eighteen years of his life there, and yet it had never really felt like home to him.

"I've traveled a lot," she said. "I've been to the West Coast, and to Europe, the Mediterranean. I lived in Israel for a while. But I've never been to Idaho, or Montana, or the Dakotas, any of those states out there."

His smile widened. "I like the way you lump Idaho and the Dakotas together."

"I know they aren't interchangeable, but they all conjure up images of great open spaces in my mind. Breathtaking vistas, clear skies, brave pioneers taming the frontier and all that."

"They've got plenty of open space, I'll grant you that."

His caustic tone seemed to discourage her. He almost apologized. Just because he didn't choose to wax poetic about his native region didn't mean she couldn't.

Idaho seemed to have lost interest for her, however. The buzz of the engine filled the cabin. The plane lurched slightly as they hit another pocket of turbulence, then lurched again.

She checked the controls before her, her frown deepening. "Damn."

He sensed more than saw the change in her demeanor. She sat straighter, her hands tight on the wheel, her lips pressed together. The plane lurched once more. She glanced at the dials and swore.

"What?"

"I think we have a problem."

He sat straighter, as well. The needles and dials cluttering the control panel held no meaning for him. The plane remained aloft, the wooded mountains far below them.

She jiggled the throttle. The plane trembled. "Would you hold these?" she asked, whipping off her sunglasses and tossing them at him. She tore off her gloves next, and he automatically took them from her.

Then she adjusted the mouthpiece on her headset and demanded contact with the control tower at the airport in Laconia. Her gaze shuttled back and forth between the windshield and a gauge on the control panel.

"What's the problem?" Judd asked.

"An oil leak. A bad one. See that needle? That's our oil pressure."

The needle was creeping counterclockwise. "What does it mean?"

"It means we've got a problem."

The plane continued to tremble. Judd focused on her fingers, on the smooth pale skin across her knuckles, her round, unpolished nails. Her voice remained soft and mellifluous as she spoke to the control tower, whose response he couldn't hear. Phrases like "oil leak" and "zero pressure" and "request emergency landing" emerged from her with eerie calm.

He observed her and measured the violent increase in the plane's vibrations. The plane swooped down and Alana wrestled it back up again. The wheel jerked against her hands.

"A Beechcraft A-90," she spoke into the mouthpiece. "Can you track me in? How far from the airport am I? Is there someplace closer we can try for?"

He heard a chugging sound. The plane dipped sideways. Alana struggled to right it. "We're on one engine now," she said into the mouthpiece.

Her fingers curled tighter around the wheel. The plane jittered and stuttered. "Plymouth? Is there a landing strip there? How close are we?" She listened for a moment. "Okay, if I take it...no, I can't see the lake from here. How far are we from Plymouth? I've got to take it down. I've lost an engine, and I've got no pressure at all." She listened. "One passenger. There's just the two of us."

Judd tried to summon up some panic, yet her poised bearing didn't leave room for hysterics on his part. A strange fatalism stole over him. He was in a small, malfunctioning plane somewhere above the White Mountains of New Hampshire, and they were going to go down.

She was reciting numbers into her mouthpiece, altitude readings, pressure readings. "There's a clearing," she muttered under her breath. "I'm going to go for it. Laconia Tower," she said into the microphone, her steadiness astonishing Judd, "we're going to ditch in a clearing. We can't make it to an airstrip. I've got to take it down now, while I've still got some power to work with."

He squinted ahead, searching for the clearing. He saw it in the distance, a swatch of white snow surrounded by green.

If they hit the trees, they'd die. If they hit the clearing, they'd probably die, too.

He was going to die with this woman.

He gazed at her, memorizing her cleanly sculpted profile, her full lips, her dark, tragic eyes. The wheel shook wildly in her left hand; her right worked the throttle, trying to keep the remaining engine alive. The plane descended, then rose again, dizzily, staggering toward the clearing.

"Grab your ankles," she ordered him.

"What?"

"Grab your ankles. Double over and protect your head. We're going down."

Judd Singer was not an emotional man. But at that instant, as the finality of his existence burned through him, he wanted to say something emotional—that he forgave her, that he admired her, that she was the most courageous woman he'd ever met.

But it was too late. The plane slammed into the snow, bounced, skidded and spun and impaled the earth in a thunder of tearing metal and crunching glass.

And then there was nothing but blackness.

Chapter Two

The first thing he saw when he opened his eyes was her sunglasses. They lay atop the instep of his right boot, one lens cracked, the frame bent.

He tried to inhale deeply, but his lungs refused to fill with air. Something compressed his ribs, forcing his breath to come in short, faint gasps.

His knees. He was still doubled over, and his knees were jammed against his chest.

He closed his eyes and sighed. A frightening silence surrounded him.

Opening his eyes once more, he slowly, cautiously straightened up. He tested his limbs, flexed his jaw. Nothing more serious than a few twinges and aches.

The silence was broken by the ghostly whistle of the wind and the creaking of trees. Looking up, he discovered that the airplane's windshield was gone. He turned to his right. The door at his elbow had remained intact. Beyond it stretched an unscathed wing.

It took him another long minute to piece together what had happened. They had crashed. They'd fallen out of the sky. He had heard the nightmare report of metal crashing and ripping into the snow. If those deathly sounds hadn't come from his side of the plane, they must have come from hers.

He was good at accepting reality, but at that moment he wanted to run as fast as he could from it. He wanted to believe, he wanted fairy tales to come true, he wanted everything perfect. He wanted to turn and find Alana smiling, dusting the broken glass from her jacket and explaining to him, in that supple, soothing voice of hers, how they were going to get themselves picked up and taken to Boston.

He wanted to trust in miracles, but he couldn't. Steeling himself for the worst, he turned toward her.

He focused on her legs first. They stretched in front of her, just as they had when she'd been flying. He traced them as far as the edge of her thick denim jacket. Then he steered his gaze higher, to her hands locked around the wheel at the end of the control stick. He followed her arms to her shoulders, to her head resting against the caved-in door on her side. Beyond the broken window he saw nothing but a sweeping drift of snow.

Her skin was as white as the snow, as peaceful, as lovely. Her headset was askew, the mouthpiece pressed into her lower lip. Her head was turned toward him, and he could see a gash of red slanted above her left brow, a narrow thread of blood trickling down to her temple and matting in her hair. A purple welt swelled below her left eye.

Her nostrils quivered slightly. She was breathing.

He yanked open his seat belt and rose onto his knees above her. Reaching past her through the shattered side window, he grabbed a fistful of snow and brought it to her cheek.

The snow melted against his fingertips, against her smooth, pale skin. After lifting the headset off her and flinging it aside, he rubbed the frozen water over her lips, over the bruise the mouthpiece had left there. Then up again, along her livid cheekbone and over her temple to wash the cut above her eyebrow. The icy crystals grew pink as they thawed and mingled with her blood.

He reached through the nonexistent window again, scooping up more fresh snow and bringing it to her face. "Alana," he said, bowing over her motionless body, rubbing the snow across her forehead, down the uninjured side of her face, over her lips again, over her chin to her throat. He took another handful of snow as he murmured her name. "Alana. Come on, open your eyes. Alana. Open your eyes."

Her lips moved against his fingers, pursing and parting in the shape of a kiss. Under any other circumstance, he would have found the motion incredibly erotic.

"Open your eyes, Alana. It's okay. Come back now, Alana. Come on back."

Her eyelids twitched, her dense black lashes fluttering. She opened her eyes. Seeing them, so profoundly dark and startled and *alive,* caused something inside Judd to fist up, a fierce, painful joy seizing his soul. He had done nothing special, yet he felt as if he'd somehow brought her back from the dead.

The emotions rampaging through him frightened him even more than the plane crash had. He shoved them down, someplace where he wouldn't have to deal with them, and gave Alana a reserved smile. He dipped his hand into the snow again and bathed her face with the icy flakes. "Do you know who you are?" he asked

She moved her lips in that unintentionally sensual way again, then swallowed. "Alana Halpern," she whispered.

"Do you know who I am?"

"Judd." Not Mr. Singer, Judd. He liked that.

"Do you know where you are?"

She closed her eyes and let out a bleak laugh that sounded suspiciously like a sob. "I'm so sorry, I—"

"Shh." He ran his cold, wet fingers over her mouth to silence her. "You saved our lives. Don't apologize."

"No, I—I couldn't... I couldn't..."

"You saved our lives," he repeated, stroking her cheeks, her trembling throat, the feverish skin of her neck. "Don't be sorry."

He rubbed his thumbs in light circles against her temples until her eyes opened again. "Can you move?" he asked.

Letting go of the wheel, she curled and straightened her fingers. He enveloped her hands in his, telling himself he only wanted to warm them but knowing he needed to hold her, to reassure not just her but himself. "How about your feet?"

She shifted her knees and shuffled her feet.

"Good," he said, closing his hands more snugly around hers. Her face was just a couple of inches below his. Her dark eyes drew him in. They shimmered with tears, with terror and profound relief. Her tongue skimmed her lips, capturing the droplets of water left by the melted snow.

Judd experienced an inappropriate but very real pang of desire.

Pulling back, he released her hands. His response was an outgrowth of fear, that was all. He'd been frightened, and she was an attractive woman, and without realizing it, she had moved her mouth in an alluring way. That was all it was.

"Where does it hurt?" he asked.

"My cheek."

"It's bruised." He pressed his finger lightly over the discolored flesh to feel for swelling. Her skin felt like that of a peach freshly washed, velvet-soft and moist. When she didn't shriek or flinch at his gentle touch, he figured it safe to assume the bone underneath wasn't fractured. "Does anything else hurt? Anything internal?"

She averted her gaze. He wondered whether his question had embarrassed her—or whether she was aware of that brief, powerful stab of passion he'd felt with her hands sandwiched between his and her lips so close to his.

"I'm all right," she said.

He guided her backward until her head rested against the broken door. "You're bleeding," he told her, groping in his pocket for a handkerchief. He folded it into a neat pad, then pressed it to her forehead.

"Oh, God," she moaned. "Is it deep?"

"I don't think so." He lifted her hand to hold the compress so he wouldn't have to risk touching her face again. Enclosed within the mangled cockpit with her, he felt raw, half-crazed with worry about her well-being, overflowing with the longing to console her and that nagging, inexcusable desire every time he glimpsed her eyes, her mouth, her long, long legs.

"There's a first aid kit," she said.

He looked around, grateful for a reason to stop gazing at her. "Where?"

"I don't know. In the back of the plane. I know there was one when I left this morning. I always ask, and they said..."

"The back of the plane," he repeated, staring at what was left of the fuselage. His duffel sat on the dented floor behind his seat, next to it a large metal toolbox. On Alana's side the wall was sheared in two, as if someone had used a sardine-can key on it. Where the tail should have been, there was only a gaping hole.

He reached behind his seat and dragged the toolbox forward. In it was an assortment of basic tools and a Red Cross first aid kit. He moistened a cotton swab with alcohol and pulled his handkerchief away from her brow. "This is going to sting," he warned.

She remained motionless as he cleaned the cut. He knew it had to hurt, yet she didn't make a sound.

He worked quickly, ignoring the lovely texture of her skin, the silky black waves of her hair. He tore open a wrapped sterile gauze pad, arranged it over the cut, and then used his teeth to break the adhesive tape into strips.

"There," he said, smoothing the tapes into place and leaning back. "How's that?"

She touched the bandage cautiously, her gaze never leaving him. "Thank you."

He dropped his bloodstained handkerchief on the floor with her twisted sunglasses. They were souvenirs of something he'd rather not be reminded of. "You rest. I'm going out to take a look around."

"No!" Her voice emerged in a soft, tortured wail.

He focused on the door, his means of escape. "I won't be gone long."

"Let me come with you."

"No. You take it easy. I'll be back." He shoved open the door beside his seat and climbed out of the plane. Sinking down into the shin-deep snow, he struggled to figure out why he felt he had to flee from her.

He had survived the crash. Yet he knew that if he spent one more minute in the demolished cabin with her, peering into her haunted eyes and drowning in her anguish, her need, her immeasurable courage...he would be lost forever.

CLOSING HER EYES, she shivered. The cabin was shockingly cold. It took her a moment to realize that the windows were broken and the wind was howling through.

She mentally reran what had happened to her, where she'd been during those few strange seconds before Judd had dragged her back to consciousness. She recalled seeing a light, small and distant, as if it were shining at her through the narrow end of a funnel.

She'd felt drawn to the light. But the sides of the funnel were so steeply sloped she couldn't navigate it.

She'd wanted to reach the light, but someone behind her had implored her to come back. He'd called her name over and over and told her to come back.

Judd Singer.

She knew what the light was, and the long, slippery funnel. She'd read articles about near-death experiences. None of the articles had said that moving toward the light would be so difficult. Maybe the funnel had been too steep for her because it hadn't yet been her time to die.

Judd Singer clearly hadn't thought it had been. He'd kept calling her, calling her back.

Who was he? A taciturn stranger, a businessman, a client her boss was trying to win over. An Idaho native. Someone who was willing to lure her back from the edge of death and then get the hell away from her, clearing out of the damaged cockpit as quickly as he could.

Tears seeped through her lashes. She'd crashed a plane. She had been trained to deal with calamities, and somewhere in her muddled brain she understood that she had handled this disaster as best she could. The oil leak hadn't been her fault, and she'd managed to keep one engine functioning long enough to land the damned aircraft, and she'd found a field of snow to put it down in, and her passenger had emerged from the ordeal without so much as a scratch.

But logic couldn't overpower the dread that gnawed at her. She'd gone down.

This was no way to impress a client. Mark Neeley was going to be furious.

She allowed herself a feeble laugh at the thought of her boss's apoplectic reaction to the news that, rather than talking up the company to a potential client, she had very nearly killed the poor man. Laughing hurt so much she started to cry again. Every part of her body ached. Every bone and joint seemed sore, her cartilage jarred, her muscles pulled and strained. And her face... bleeding, stinging, disfigured for life.

Worst of all, she was bawling like a helpless baby, wanting nothing more than Judd's hands stroking her once more, bathing her skin, consoling her. She wanted him to stay with her and make her all better.

What if he never came back? What if he blamed her for the crash? He was in good shape; maybe he'd marched off, ostensibly to search for help but in fact just trying to put some distance between himself and his blundering, blubbering pilot.

She had to get up. She had to get out of the plane before she went crazy.

She tried to sit and couldn't.

"Oh God, oh God, oh God," she murmured, her teeth chattering. She couldn't sit up.

"Judd!" She screamed as loud as she could. She didn't care if she sounded insane, if her voice echoed through the mountain range, through the entire state of New Hampshire. She didn't care. She couldn't remain another instant trapped inside the plane and unable to move. "Judd!"

She heard the rapid tread of footsteps breaking through the crisp surface of the snow. He poked his head inside the open doorway, his cheeks ruddy and his breath emerging in thick clouds of vapor. "What's wrong?" he asked, kneeling on the seat and scrutinizing her.

"I can't sit up."

He rubbed his hands together to warm them, then slid closer to her on the seat. "Your seat belt's still on," he said.

"Oh." Feeling absurdly stupid, she fumbled with the buckle. He nudged her hands away and unclasped the belt himself. She winced at the sudden, searing pain that sluiced across her abdomen.

"What?" he asked.

She was not going to cry anymore. "It's all right," she said in a tight voice.

"You're hurt."

"No. It's all right."

Disregarding her claim, he shifted to make room for her legs, which he eased out from under the control panel and stretched across his seat. Without a word, he pulled back the flaps of her jacket, his hands decisive and businesslike, his gaze riveted to her hips and his thin lips pressed into a straight line. She shut her eyes, unable to watch as he rolled up the hem of her Fair Isle sweater, opened the fly of her corduroy slacks and pushed her turtleneck out of his way. He was as dispassionate as a physician, yet she couldn't bear to see him touching her.

Until she heard him suck in his breath. Then she couldn't bear *not* to see. She propped herself up on her elbows, high enough to notice the grotesque violet blotches underlining the curve of her belly.

"Lie down," he ordered her.

"The seat belt . . ."

"It's probably just a bruise. Lie down."

She did. She stared at the warped ceiling above her as he pressed his flattened palm against her belly. His hand was large, covering a wide area. She remembered how strong it had felt when they'd shaken hands at the terminal.

It felt stronger now, warm and firm yet amazingly gentle. He slid it an inch lower and pressed again, sending ripples of sensation through her body.

"What are you doing?" she asked, mortified by the tremor in her voice.

"Palpating." He moved his hand and pressed again, quietly probing.

"What are you, a doctor?"

"My father's a doctor. My mother's a nurse." He slid his hand lower, against the elastic trim of her panties, and pressed again. If her brain was functioning normally, she would slap him for daring to touch her so brazenly. Or else she would writhe and gasp and beg him to touch her again, lower, harder . . .

Instead, she kept her gaze pinned to the ceiling. *Pretend he isn't a hunk of blue-eyed, tawny-haired masculinity,* she ordered herself. *Pretend he's his father, the doctor. Better yet, pretend he's his mother, the nurse.*

"What are you feeling for?" she asked.

A dry laugh escaped him. "Damned if I know. But if something was really wrong you'd be screaming."

She was close to screaming now—only not from pain. His fingertips had stretched down to explore the soft flesh beneath her panties. It hurt the way any severe bruise would hurt, but she tuned out the pain and concentrated on what truly mattered: Did he think she was fat? Did he think her beige cotton bikini panties were boring? Did he find this entire exercise incredibly embarrassing, or even distasteful?

"I'm okay," she insisted, suddenly desperate for him to remove his hands from her.

"I think so." Evidently he felt just as desperate to end the examination. He tugged down her turtleneck, pulled up her slacks and zipped the fly with uncommon speed. Only when she was fully clothed did he dare to lean toward her, gripping her upper arms and helping her into a sitting position.

She groaned. Perhaps she was okay, but her hips and abdomen hurt, and so did her head. And her chin. And her left arm. And her cheek. The truth of her predicament bludgeoned her until she fell toward him in a swoon.

He caught her, cradled her against his chest and ran his hands comfortingly through her hair. "Easy does it."

She waited until the tiny pinpricks of black cleared from her vision. "You go get help," she mumbled, burying her face against the worn leather of his jacket. "I'll just lie down and die."

"Not a chance."

"That was a joke."

"Oh."

His fingers slid under her hair to the nape of her neck and massaged the base of her skull. She relived the sensation of his hand on her belly, the strength of

it, the provocative heat of his skin gliding over hers.
She shuddered and he tightened his hold on her for a
minute.

Then he released her and carefully withdrew.
"There's a shack."

"What?"

He pulled back far enough for her to see him.
"There's a shack not far from the clearing. I'm going
to take the tool chest and break in."

"Break in? Like a burglar?"

Her comment seemed to amuse him. "Maybe we'll
get lucky and someone will come along to arrest us,"
he said, backing to the door and lifting her onto his
seat, which was in better condition than hers.

"Do you know how to break and enter?"

"Sure," he said, hauling the toolbox from behind
the seat. "Harry Houdini used to be my idol. If he
could pick a lock, so can I." He stepped out of the
plane, then peered in through the open doorway. His
eyes were crystalline, his gaze moving over her with
laser precision. "You rest. I'll come back for you."

"Promise?"

"Promise." Hovering in the doorway, he seemed to
be on the verge of saying something more, but all he
did was reach out and run his thumb lightly over the
gauze bandage, smoothing the tape that held it to her
forehead. Then he turned and slammed the door
against the brisk December wind.

Shutting her eyes, she nestled into the seat, ignoring the pain and the nausea, ignoring the unwanted
tears that once again threatened to swamp her. She
concentrated on the sensation of his thumb against her

brow, his fingers at the back of her neck, his hand kneading the soft flesh above her pelvis. She concentrated on his piercing blue eyes.

He would come back. He'd promised. And her tears vanished, unspent.

IT WASN'T MUCH—an old hunter's cabin in the woods, more a hovel than a sporting lodge. When he'd stumbled onto it in a grove of alder, birch and white pine, he had immediately searched for a road, another cabin, any sign of human life. Whatever road led to it was obscured by the snow, and the only other building he found was an outhouse a short hike through the trees. A small overhang jutting out from the rough-hewn wall beside the cabin door sheltered a stack of perhaps a dozen split logs. The door was held shut with a simple hardware store padlock.

He rummaged through the tool chest for a narrow file, which he jammed into the key hole. *Not as much showmanship as Harry Houdini,* he thought. But then, he didn't have an audience.

After a few tries, the lock sprang open.

The hinges creaked as the door gave against the weight of his shoulder. The cabin was dim and musty. The afternoon light had to sift through the forest and the dusty window panes to illuminate the single room. Judd's footsteps echoed hollowly on the plank floor as he ventured inside.

Nearest the door was the living area—a circular pine table and four ladder-back chairs, an old rocker next to one of the windows, a gun rack on the wall with two rifles hanging on it. Farther into the room was what passed for a kitchen: a cement dry sink, a large wood-burning stove, a work counter and plenty of cabinets. At the far end of the room stood two cots, parallel to each other against opposite walls, with a dresser between them. The cots were stripped, their black-and-white striped mattresses resting crookedly on the steel frames.

It would do.

He opened a few cabinets, a few drawers, unearthing linens and blankets, pots, a bottle of whisky, crackers and pretzels, paper towels, dishes and silverware. In one cabinet he found a large kerosene lamp, next to it a nearly empty bottle of lamp oil. Under one of the cots he found a large washbasin.

The cabin was cold, but certainly no colder than the ravaged hull of the airplane. As soon as he got Alana settled, he would build a fire and warm up the room.

He pulled a sheet from one of the dresser drawers. Wrinkling his nose at the camphor smell, he shook it out and made up one of the cots quickly, efficiently, refusing to let himself picture Alana in it. He was doing this because he was a human being, not because the sight of those ugly bruises below her belly had sickened him and made him wish he were a real magician, able to make her pain disappear with a flick and a flourish. Why couldn't he have been the injured one, instead? Why did it have to be her? What had she done to deserve it?

She had flown the plane, that was what. She had kept her head up and her hands on the controls, instead of bending over and protecting herself. She had saved their lives—which only made her injuries even more unfair.

He recalled the heat of her skin against his hand. He recalled the creamy flesh below her waist, the dainty indentation of her navel, the curving edge of her underpants, the darker, nastier bruises at her hipbones where her seat belt had dug in the worst. He recalled the way her breath had caught as he'd felt for swelling beneath the surface of her skin, and the way his own heart had raced. He'd told himself at the time that it was only concern for her health that made his pulse pound so hard.

He had examined her the way his father used to examine people—with clinical detachment. If he'd felt her tears too personally, it was because, unlike his father, he wasn't a professional.

And if he spent an inordinate amount of time smoothing out the sheet on the cot and spreading the thickest blanket on top of it, it was only because he wanted her to be comfortable.

He turned down the blanket, then dug his chilly hands into his pockets and strode out of the cabin.

Seeing the demolished plane in the clearing was as horrifying this time as it had been when he'd first climbed out and viewed the wreckage. The tail of the plane lay in scattered chunks across the field, leaving a ragged hole at the rear of the cabin. The left wing had torn clear off the fuselage and come to rest amid a cluster of trees. The cabin lay at an angle, the nose covered with snow. On his way to the passenger door, he had to step over a severed piece of the landing gear, and then a trail of shredded rubber from the disintegrated tire.

He didn't believe in miracles...except that he couldn't figure out any other way to explain how he and Alana had survived such an accident.

He found her where he'd left her, propped up in the passenger seat, looking pale but calm. When he opened the door she glanced up at him. Her eyes mystified him with their dark, searing beauty. The red welt under her lower lip had faded, making the bruise along her cheekbone look more vivid in comparison.

"Just slide forward," he said, leaning in and bracing her arms with his hands. "I'll carry you to the cabin."

"Don't be silly. I can walk."

Her obvious annoyance reassured him. But when she tried to stand her legs buckled, and before she could argue he had her in his arms.

"I'm too heavy," she said as he lifted her higher, sliding one arm under her knees and arching the other around her shoulders.

"No, you're not." He turned and started hiking back to the cabin.

"Let me see the plane," she said.

He hesitated. The gruesome sight might upset her. He wasn't by nature overly protective, yet he wanted to protect her.

She clearly didn't want him to. "Let me see it," she demanded.

Sighing, he turned until she could view what remained of the small aircraft. She let out a startled cry, proving that he'd been right to want to spare her. But when he started to turn back toward the cabin, she tightened her grip on his shoulder and craned her neck. "Where's the other wing?"

"It got stuck in some trees," he said, walking toward the rear of the hulk so she could see. "It tore right off."

She stared at the detached wing, the disconnected tail. He felt the tension in her, in the way her fingers pinched the nape of his neck and her spine stiffened. After a minute she closed her eyes and let out a long breath. "The snow," she said. "The snow saved us. It kept the engines from exploding on impact."

"*You* saved us," he said.

"No," she refuted him without a trace of false modesty. "It was the snow."

Out of respect for her weakened state, he chose not to continue the debate. He turned and slogged through the field of snow, following the trail of his own footsteps toward the shack. She lowered her head to his shoulder, and he caught a whiff of her herbal shampoo.

"We should do something," she said.

"Hmm?"

"With the plane. We should clear off the snow so it'll be more visible from the air. They'll be using helicopters to search for us. We should—"

"I'll take care of it."

"No, really, Judd—it's my responsibility. I'm the pilot. If you'll just put me down…"

The way her head rested against his shoulder, the way her hand relaxed at the back of his neck and her body nestled into his arms, he suspected she wasn't all that eager to be put down. "I'll take care of it," he said, kicking the cabin door open and stalking inside.

She lifted her head to look around as he crossed to the bed he'd made up for her. Carefully, he lowered her onto the thin mattress. Her head sank into the pillow and she groaned softly.

He started to remove her jacket, then thought better of it and removed her shoes, instead. He'd prefer if she took off her own jacket. He had already spent too much time in close proximity to her enticing body.

But she didn't touch her jacket. She reached for the blanket and started to draw it up over her.

"Take your jacket off," he ordered her.

"It's cold."

"I'm going to build a fire. Take your jacket off."

She started to, then whimpered as she tried to shrug out of the sleeves.

He clamped his hands over hers to keep her from moving. "What?"

"Nothing," she said through gritted teeth.

He felt her fingers stirring against his palms, trying to wriggle free. "Where does it hurt?"

"I'm all right."

He eased the sleeves of the jacket down her arms. "Where?"

She sighed in defeat. "My left shoulder. It's just a little sore, that's all."

He considered the situation. To examine her shoulder would require removing her sweater and turtleneck completely. He really ought to check her arm; something could be dislocated or broken. Yet he'd barely recovered from his first encounter with what lurked beneath her clothing.

Opting for safety, he left her sweater in place and clamped one hand over her shoulder, the other around her elbow. He rotated her arm until she yelped in pain.

"I'm sure it's just sprained or something," she said through clenched teeth.

"You could be badly hurt, Alana."

"It's just a sprain." She nudged him away and lay down.

Her complexion was ashen and her hands shook slightly. He spread the blanket over her. "There's a pile of wood outside," he told her. "I'll bring some in and get the fire going."

She pulled the blanket up to her chin and nodded.

He was glad to be busy, gathering a few split logs and kindling and making the fire. "The room will start warming up soon," he said.

She nodded.

She looked so small and frail curled up under the blanket. He wished he could do more—wave a magic wand and turn the room into a tropical paradise, complete with a medical staff to tend to her wounds. Barring that, he wished she would complain a bit. Her stoicism only made him feel guiltier that she'd gotten hurt and he hadn't.

He pulled the basin from underneath the other cot. "I'm going to fill this with snow and melt it down. We haven't got any water here."

"And then I'll help you clear off the plane."

"You're going to rest," he corrected her. "I'll clear off the plane."

"You need to brush the snow away from the wing markings, Judd. And you should decorate the site with something colorful so it'll be visible from the air."

"I'll take care of it."

"You can use my scarf."

"You might need your scarf." He opened one of the drawers and pulled out a red plaid blanket, then held it out for her approval.

"Okay."

He moved to the door with the blanket and the basin. "Try to get some rest."

By the time he came back with the snow-filled basin, she was asleep.

He set it atop the stove to melt. He wasn't sure what they'd need all that water for, but he figured it made sense to have a supply on hand.

A good hour must have elapsed since Alana's last communication with the control tower in Laconia; helicopters ought to be scouting the area soon. Judd would make the wreckage as visible as possible. Surely he and Alana would be rescued before they would ever need fresh water.

He studied the basin, shook his head, and moved it closer to the fire box. The realist in him was kicking in. He and Alana had already exhausted their ration of luck when they'd survived the crash. Hoping for a quick rescue was futile.

He observed her. She was snuggled under the blanket, her hair splayed out on the pillow, her eyelashes shaping two thick black crescents against her cheeks. He looked at the discoloration below her left eye, and the bandage above it, then her full pink lips and the fragile line of her jaw.

Judd Singer was not a pushover. Or a softie. He didn't like women who acted helpless.

Maybe that was what was getting to him: Alana might be banged up and battered, dizzy and weak, but she was far from helpless. A short laugh escaped him. Even half-asleep on the cot, she'd been issuing commands.

His laughter waned as he remembered the way her skin had felt against his fingertips. The way her breath had caught as his hand had moved across her abdomen. The way he'd felt her pain as if it were his own. The way he'd felt reborn the moment she'd opened her eyes to him.

He didn't like it. He didn't like the effect she had on him. Merely being with her made him feel as if he were in the plane once more, going down, going down and unable to save himself.

Armed with the bright plaid blanket, he left the cabin and headed through the snowy woods to the wreckage, hoping that someone would rescue them before it was too late.

Chapter Three

By four o'clock the sky had turned from clear blue to mauve as the sun slipped below the mountains' western slopes, spreading long shadows across the snow. Alana picked her way carefully along the vaguely defined path to the cabin, carrying the jar of lime and the roll of toilet paper she'd found in a cabinet.

She'd awakened to find herself alone in the cabin. Pretending she didn't ache with each movement, she'd gotten out of bed and surveyed her surroundings. Her mind had clarified itself. She was alive, and for the time being she was safe. Judd had brought her here. He had bathed her and bandaged her and carried her to this shack, this haven.

And then he'd left.

What was it about him? How could he be so attentive one minute and so remote the next? Was disappearing at the drop of a hat one of his magic tricks?

Fate had thrown him and Alana together, and she supposed he was doing his best under the circumstances. His best was to keep her from bleeding and passing out in the snow. It wasn't to be her friend.

Judd Singer was who he was; she would simply have to accept it. Sooner or later they would be rescued, and then—if he was irrational enough to choose Neeley, Henderson—she would have only the most minimal, professional contact with him. She didn't need to like or understand him. She simply needed to coexist with him until someone found them.

And she needed to pretend she wasn't the least bit aware of how handsome he was.

The jar of lime and a roll of toilet paper in a cabinet had told her there must be an outhouse somewhere. She'd pulled on her jacket, cursing at the throbbing in her left shoulder, and then headed outside.

She was more than halfway back to the cabin when she spotted Judd Singer jogging toward her from the clearing, his boots kicking up sprays of snow. "What are you doing up?" he asked.

She held up the toilet paper.

"You should have waited for me."

"Maybe I couldn't wait."

His hair was mussed, his cheeks and nose red from the cold. His eyes were clear, though. She read contrition in their glittering blue depths.

She could have reassured him that she wasn't an invalid, and that she didn't blame him for not being there to escort her to the outhouse. But she didn't feel like reassuring him. She was thoroughly annoyed by the way he kept doting on her and then vanishing, doting and vanishing. She wished he'd do one or the other—stick by her or steer clear of her.

"Lucky for me I'm all right," she muttered, resuming her slow, faltering walk back to the cabin. "Who knows what would have happened if I had to count on you?"

If she'd hoped to rouse anger in him, she had obviously failed. He fell into step next to her, his hand hovering near her elbow but not taking it. His face remained impassive. "I was trying to make the plane visible from above," he said evenly, not a trace of defensiveness in his tone. "I checked on you a few times. You were fast asleep."

She glanced at him. He stared at the cabin, avoiding her eyes.

So he cared enough to check on her. He cared enough to usher her back to the cabin. Once she was inside, he would probably disappear again.

The shadows stretched longer; the sky grew grayer. "If we aren't found soon, they're going to call off their search for the night," she commented grimly.

"Can't they use spotlights?"

She shrugged, then bit her lip at the stab of pain that simple gesture produced. "If they haven't found us by now, they're probably searching in the wrong place. Did any helicopters fly overhead?"

"No. I heard what sounded like one."

"You did?"

"I didn't see it, though. I guess it didn't see me, either." He pushed open the cabin door and waved her in ahead of him.

"What did you do to make the plane visible?"

"Cleared away the snow and tied the blanket to the wing."

She couldn't think of anything else that would attract a helicopter, at least not this late in the day. "I guess we're stuck here till tomorrow, then," she said, heading directly for one of the chairs before her legs gave out.

Judd helped her take off her jacket then went to inspect the fire. It was blazing merrily.

She gazed at the dancing golden flames. They reminded her of other flames, happy fires, a celebration of warmth and light and love. A doleful sigh escaped her.

Judd peered over his shoulder at her. "What?"

"Nothing."

He seemed to consider questioning her further, then decided against it. He moved around the counter to a cabinet near the sink and pulled down the kerosene lamp and the bottle of oil. "We ought to get this lit," he said, dumping the meager contents of the oil bottle into the well of the lamp. "It'll be dark soon."

His words settled on her like the darkness itself, heavy and gloomy. She sighed again.

He screwed the wick into place and straightened up. "What?"

"Hanukkah." She rested her chin in her hands and stared past him at the stove. "Tonight's the first night of Hanukkah."

He mulled over her statement, then lit the wick.

"I don't expect that to mean anything to you," she went on when he didn't speak. "Just try to imagine how you'd feel if it was Christmas Eve. Well, maybe not Christmas Eve. People tend to equate Christmas with Hanukkah because they come at the same time of

year, but actually, Hanukkah's more like...I'm not
sure what Christian holiday it's like. It isn't about
getting toys or anything, it's about—"

"I know."

She watched as he set the glass chimney back in
place. The wick burned an intense white, casting a
halo of light around the lamp. Judd carried it to the
table.

She eyed him distrustfully. She didn't want false
sympathy from him. She was missing her holiday tonight, missing it all—the songs, the dreidel games, the
foil-covered chocolate coins, her mother's special
feast, her niece's sticky kisses, her nephew's first Hanukkah. She was missing her family, her home. The
warmth and light and love.

The hell with her cuts and scrapes and bruises. *This*
was what hurt.

"I really don't think you understand," she said,
gazing toward the window and watching dismally as
night descended over the forest.

Judd strode to the door. "I do understand," he
said, opening it and stepping outside.

"Now you see him, now you don't," she mumbled
under her breath. The magician of the Magic Shops
was doing his disappearing act once again.

But just as quickly he was back, carrying a couple
of split logs for the fire. He kicked the door shut behind him and ambled to the stove, where he added one
log and left the other on the floor for later.

"Are you hungry?" he asked, shedding his jacket
and throwing it onto the rocker.

If he understood anything at all about what she was feeling, he wouldn't be asking her if she was hungry. "Sure, I'm hungry," she railed. "I'm hungry for a great big feast and lots of icky-sweet kosher wine. But I don't expect you—"

"I understand," he snapped. "I'm Jewish, too. Okay?"

She gaped at him, at his tall, rugged build, at his open leather jacket and long denim-clad legs, at his uncanny blue eyes. "How can you be Jewish?" she blurted out. "You're from Idaho."

He issued a short, humorless laugh. "And I hate sweet wine. How about whisky?" He pulled a bottle from a cabinet below the counter and a couple of glasses from a cabinet above it.

"We can't drink that. It isn't ours."

Judd's response was to pour an inch of whisky into one of the glasses and down it in a few swallows. Then he refilled his glass and poured a shot into the other glass. "I'll leave some money."

"It isn't good to drink on an empty stomach."

He set a glass of whisky in front of her. "Are you hungry?" he asked again.

"Look, it's Hanukkah, all right? The Festival of Lights. We ought to do something special before we eat."

"We did," he said. "We crashed a plane."

"I'm glad you think this is funny. Maybe in Idaho, Hanukkah is an occasion for sick jokes. Where I come from, it's a holy day. It's a celebration."

"Okay. Let's celebrate surviving the plane crash." He lifted his glass in a toast.

She studied him in the lamplight. What if he got drunk? He might black out. Or worse. They were alone in the mountains, she had no means of escape, she was already in a weakened condition....

And he had tended to her wounds with care and compassion. If he had wanted to do something awful to her, he would have done it by now. As long as he could handle his booze, she would be safe with him.

She couldn't deny that surviving the crash was worth celebrating. Smiling meekly, she clinked her glass against Judd's and took a sip.

The whisky seared her throat and chest. She shuddered as its potency sizzled through her. "That is *not* icky-sweet kosher wine."

"Thank God."

She sent him a thoughtful look. "We *should* thank God."

Judd settled into his seat, stretching his legs under the table and hooking one arm over the back of the chair. "Go ahead."

She scanned the room and pushed herself out of her chair. "We need a candle. Actually, we need a menorah, but that's asking too much."

In a trice Judd was on his feet, circling the table and nudging her back into her chair. "Sit."

"I'm all right, Judd."

Ignoring her protest, he carried the lamp to the kitchen and began a quest for a candle. Eventually he located a stub of a utility candle, thick and white, along with an ashtray. He softened one end of the candle over the stove and planted it firmly in the center of the ashtray. "There," he said. "There's your menorah."

She thought of the beautiful brass candelabrum in her parents' house. It was an heirloom; her father's grandmother had brought it to America from her village in Russia just after the turn of the century. Generations of polish had kept it bright and shiny; generations of love and affection had greeted its display every December.

She stared at the fat white candle in the ashtray and resisted the urge to weep. "Right now," she said, "my mother is probably chewing me out in absentia for not getting to her house in time for the candle lighting."

"Right now," Judd corrected her quietly, "your mother is probably on the phone with every airport and police department in New England, trying to find out what happened to you."

He was right—and his vision of her parents was far worse than hers.

It agonized her to think her parents would be worrying. If only she could call them, could let them know she was safe. That she was sheltered for the night in a mountain hut with a wood-burning stove and two separate beds for her and her passenger.

Judd pressed the matchbox into her hand. She tore her gaze from the candle. "Are we supposed to cover our heads?" she asked, pulling a match out of the box.

"Beats me."

She struck the match and touched it to the wick. There were words, prayers—but she didn't know them. "I'm supposed to say something."

"So say it."

"In Hebrew. I don't remember what. I never was good at Hebrew, even when I lived in Israel."

"Then say it in English." At her hesitation, he added, "Do you think God won't listen if you pray in English?"

Of course God would listen. She touched the match to the wick, bowed her head and prayed, her soft voice filling the shadowy cabin. "Blessed art Thou, oh Lord, our God, King of the Universe," she began, because that was how she remembered all Jewish prayers beginning. Bits and pieces of the Hanukkah blessing came to her: "We thank our God for the miracles He has performed. We thank Him for keeping us alive and enabling us to reach this day." She thought for a minute, then added: "Thank You for providing us with this cabin for the night, and the firewood to keep us warm."

"And the whisky," Judd added.

She shot him a quick look. His mischievous grin provoked a tentative smile from her. "And the whisky to keep us warm. Please send a rescue crew our way asap. And..." She meditated, then decided she'd touched on all the important points. "Happy Hanukkah, and I'm sorry this isn't in Hebrew. Amen." She glanced up at Judd again.

"That was good."

"You're supposed to say 'Amen.'"

"Amen."

She took another sip of the liquor. It sent a frisson of heat through her.

"You really should eat something," he said, carrying the lamp into the kitchen. "There's food here—crackers, snacks, cookies..."

"I don't feel right about stealing food."

"Chicken noodle soup," he announced, lifting a couple of cans from a shelf and setting them on the counter.

She felt her morals fraying as her stomach clenched in hunger. "I suppose it's all right...in an emergency."

"I'll leave money," he promised, rummaging through the kitchen area for a pot and a can opener. In no time, he had the soup heating on the stove.

"I feel useless just sitting here," she complained as Judd collected bowls and spoons and brought them to the table.

His only response was to head back to the kitchen for a box of crackers.

"Will your family be worried about your whereabouts?" she asked.

"Tonight? No."

That implied that he hadn't had any plans for the holiday. Even if Hanukkah didn't mean much to him, Alana still felt sorry for him. To her, the best thing about holidays was their emphasis on family, tradition, repeating the words and gestures her ancestors had given birth to thousands of years ago.

She couldn't bear to remain at the table while Judd took care of everything. Despite his posture, his aura of aloofness and his commands that she stay seated—or maybe because of them—she felt she had to get up and help. Sitting still wasn't Alana's style. Neither was taking orders from a man.

She struggled to her feet. Pain seared down her left arm, down her left leg, across her left cheek. She stared at the candle flickering at the center of the table and added a silent prayer that she wouldn't collapse and give Judd another excuse to fuss over her.

Before she could either sit back down or take a step, he was already ladling the steaming soup into the bowls. They sat across the table from each other, the area illuminated by the single utility candle.

The flame's golden radiance spread across his face, gilding the harsh edge of his chin, the shelf of his brow, the planes of his cheeks. His eyes appeared less cool than they had earlier. Cool or warm, Judd's eyes were still a riveting blue. She tried to think of what blues from her assortment of paints she would have to mix on her palette to attain that color, and came up blank.

She tasted the soup and sighed. It thawed her in a much more benign way than the whisky had. "Thanks."

"I'm real good at opening cans."

"No—I mean, for letting me observe the holiday."

He spooned some soup into his mouth, his eyes never leaving her. Finally he shrugged. "It was a nice prayer."

"I couldn't remember any of the words—"

"What you said was fine."

She ate a little more soup. "This tastes good," she said.

"Chicken soup's supposed to cure you."

A dawning smile curved her lips. "You *are* Jewish, aren't you?"

"I know about chicken soup, whatever that proves." His grin softened, deepened. His gaze held hers, reaching beyond her eyes to her soul and touching her in some profound, undefinable way. Then, abruptly, he turned his attention back to his food, as if that instant of tacit communion had unnerved him.

Listening to the click of his spoon against his bowl, to the faint, guttural sound of him swallowing, the crunch of a cracker as he bit into it, she savored the momentary peace and wondered how long it would last.

AFTER DINNER he took a walk. Over Alana's protests, he'd cleaned up from their supper without any assistance from her, heating water on the stove and then cleaning the dishes in the dry sink. He'd refilled the basin with fresh snow, set it on the stove to melt, and told her he was going out.

At first she'd seemed on the verge of objecting. But instead of giving voice to the anger he saw churning in her eyes, she'd muttered, "Fine. If you fall in a snow bank I'll look for you in the morning."

He should have stayed with her. He knew he should have, and yet... Every minute he was with her he felt more tied to her, more responsible for her. He owed her his life, and that debt frightened him.

After-dinner walks were a habit left over from his childhood, when he and his father used to stroll around the neighborhood at least one evening a week. Sometimes they'd talk and sometimes not a word would pass between them. They were content just to be in each other's company.

Judd recalled strolling through the neighborhood of his youth on a chilly evening just like this one—mid-December, snow covering the front yards and heaped along the edges of the streets, the sky a collage of stars and drifting clouds. He'd been no older than seven or eight, taking two steps to his father's one, burying his hands in the pockets of his jacket just as his father did, just as he was doing now.

"Everybody's got lights but us," he'd said.

"We've got electricity, same as all the other houses."

"Not electricity, Dad. Lights. Christmas lights."

It hadn't quite been true; some of the other houses hadn't been strung with colorful lights. But even those had wreaths on their doors, ropes of holly coiling around their porch railings, manger scenes on their snow-covered lawns. Peeking through windows, Judd had spied Christmas trees decked out in tinsel and dazzling ornaments.

Every house in their sleepy working-class neighborhood of Clancy, Idaho had been decorated for Christmas but one.

"Why can't we have lights, Dad?"

"Because that's not our faith," his father had said. "We don't believe in Christmas."

Judd had wanted desperately to believe in Christmas. He'd wanted to believe what all his friends believed: that a fat, jolly man slid down your chimney and left toys for you. "Why don't we believe in it?"

His father had continued his long, brisk gait, forcing Judd to scramble to keep up. "Different people believe different things," he'd said.

Judd had been certain the Singers were the only different people in the world. "Can't we change so we believe in Christmas?"

His father had sighed. "It wouldn't matter if you changed or not. It doesn't matter what you believe. You'll always be Jewish, Judd. It's in your blood. It's who you are."

"Well, why doesn't Santa Claus leave presents for Jewish kids? I'm as good as Paul Garrity. He's always getting in trouble at school, and he gets all kinds of presents. Why can't I get presents?"

That year, his mother had decided they would celebrate Hanukkah, so Judd wouldn't feel left out. When she couldn't find a single store in Clancy that sold menorahs, she'd fashioned one out of modeling clay with birthday candle holders jammed in to hold the candles. "If you want a holiday, Judd," she'd said, "we'll make you a holiday."

He'd loved the clay menorah. It had made him feel not so much different as special. But then his friends had ridiculed it. "That's the dumbest birthday cake I ever saw!" Paul Garrity had hooted, and Robbie Sanford had sneered, "Say, Judd, can I blow out the candles and make a wish?"

He'd hated the menorah after that. He'd knocked it off the shelf, pretending it was an accident, and gleefully swept the broken pieces into the trash. When his parents gave him his presents, they didn't mean anything. They were just presents, because it was December and Judd was as good as all the other kids, and if they deserved presents so did he.

It would have been so much easier if they'd just celebrated Christmas, he'd thought. It would have been so much easier if he hadn't been different.

The night air was crisp, glazing the snow with a surface layer of ice. Judd's boots made loud crunching noises as he walked toward the clearing, toward the wrecked airplane. The red plaid blanket remained securely fastened to the unbroken wing, but Judd doubted even a helicopter spotlight would be able to locate it in the darkness.

Hanukkah, he thought, stomping through the snow to the fuselage and leaning against it. The holiday no longer had any significance for him. He'd learned the history surrounding it, but that was all—history, a tale of a battle fought and won, of a temple vandalized by marauders and restored by the victorious Jews with a little help from God. It was a legend, a myth. It had nothing to do with him.

Alana's prayer, though... That had had everything to do with him. Everything to do with them both.

He tilted his head back until he could see the sky. Stars winked through the tufted clouds. The wind soughed through the trees, draping him in its icy mantle.

If God was listening, Judd hoped Alana's prayer would be answered. Not for him but for her.

"Take care of her, okay?" he whispered into the air.

Asking for anything for himself would be selfish. He didn't need anything, except to get back to civilization, back to his life. He had a business to run, with outlets in five major cities, in the midst of the pre-Christmas rush, the most crucial time of the year for retail sales. He just wanted to get back to his apartment in Manhattan, let the ad agencies court him, let his accountant figure out the year-end profit share for his employees, and make a reservation for dinner somewhere nice for New Year's Eve. If he didn't, Susan would have a fit. She expected the best. Sometimes it seemed to take a lot to satisfy her.

Alana had been satisfied with a half-used utility candle stuck to an ashtray.

"God, rescue us both," he whispered.

He couldn't keep walking out on her, yet staying with her in that cabin was torture. When he was with her, every cell in his body was attuned to her. He scrutinized her wounds, monitored her breathing, worried about her—and knew how much she resented his concern.

Even worse, he wanted her. Sure, she was pretty, and sure, her incredible skill at the plane's controls had saved them both, and now they were stranded, just the two of them in that tiny cabin, facing a long, dark night. What man wouldn't get ideas?

Bad ideas. He couldn't let himself touch her again, couldn't let himself respond to the honeyed lilt of her voice and feel it stroking his nerve endings. He couldn't let himself gaze into her dark, lovely eyes and feel her fear, so closely mirroring his own.

He stayed outside, resting against the battered frame of the airplane, surrounded by the wind and the night and the snow.

Chapter Four

The hell with him.

If Judd Singer wanted to stay outside in the freezing cold all night, that was his business. She certainly wasn't going to sit here pining for him to come back.

Alana heaved herself out of the rocker, gritting her teeth against the daggers of pain. All those drawers and cabinets beckoned her; maybe she'd find something in them to occupy herself.

In one of them she discovered a deck of cards, a large pad of paper and a pencil. "Figures," she muttered. Hunters wouldn't have any good books lying around, but surely, after a long, hard day slaughtering Bambi look-alikes, they would want to unwind with a few rounds of poker.

She took the pad and pencil to the table and began to sketch.

How much time had passed when the squeak of the door hinges announced Judd's return she had no idea. She remained focused on her drawing, rubbing the moistened tip of her index finger over a section of shadow in the picture, smudging the pencil lines to create contour. She preferred painting over sketching—particularly sketching with something as inert as graphite. Paint was big, bright, smelly and messy. Sketching was more dignified than Alana liked.

Leaning back, she appraised her work. For a simple drawing, it wasn't bad.

Judd closed the door behind him. Refusing to glance his way, she listened to his thick-soled boots clomping on the floorboards, the metallic rasp as he unzipped his jacket, the whisper of his hands rubbing together to restore the circulation in them. When he came to a halt behind her chair, she felt his nearness along her spine. The wisps of hair at the nape of her neck bristled.

"That's us," he said, studying the sketch.

She studied it, too. She had drawn the table, with the candle at its center and Judd and herself seated across from each other. She wasn't very good at self-portraiture; she lacked the necessary objectivity. So she'd drawn her face in shadow.

She'd drawn Judd's face in shadow, as well. If she'd wanted, she could have rendered his features with photographic precision—the pale eyes, the high brow, the sturdy nose and jaw, the thin, sensuous lips. She didn't need to have him posing in front of her to know what he looked like; in the few hours they'd spent together, his appearance had been permanently engraved in her memory.

But when she was drawing a portrait, she didn't set out to convey just the features. She liked the subject's spirit to come through. And she knew absolutely nothing about Judd's spirit.

"You're very talented," he said.

She shrugged and pretended that moving her shoulder hadn't inflamed her entire arm with pain.

"Is this the sort of thing you do at Neeley, Henderson?"

She suspected that he didn't ordinarily put forth such an effort to start a conversation, and she took his attempt as a compliment. "No," she replied. "When I do art at the agency, they tell me what they need and I create it for them. When I draw for myself, it comes from inside me."

He moved to her side, leaned forward, and rested his elbows on the table. His shoulder was less than an inch from hers; her skin tingled as if he were exuding some sort of force field. Even though his gaze never veered from the drawing, she felt as though he was staring directly at her. In a way, he was.

"This—" he gestured at the sketch "—was inside you?"

She wasn't sure how to answer. "It's . . . my impression of Hanukkah."

His smile was gentle, not mocking. "It's kind of stark."

"Our celebration was kind of stark," she countered. "Someday I'll show this drawing to my children and say, 'That was the weirdest Hanukkah your mommy ever had.'"

He scrutinized the drawing for a minute longer, as if it was of vital importance. Then he straightened up and moved to the opposite end of the room, where he pulled open a dresser drawer and took out a set of bed linens.

Alana observed him as he made up the second cot. She wanted to help him but knew if she did, they'd end up arguing about whether she should be on her feet.

She didn't want to argue with him. She wanted to get through the night without hating him, without becoming obsessed with his magnificent physique, without wishing he could take her in his arms and make all her pain and dread and shame about crashing the plane go away.

Tomorrow this would be over. All she had to do was endure one night with him.

She watched him whip the blanket flat above the bed. It remained in the air, levitating for an interminable minute before it descended evenly onto the mattress.

"How did you do that?" she asked.

He shot her a bemused glance. "Do what?"

"Make the blanket stay in the air like that."

He surveyed the bed, then shrugged and crossed to the basin of melted snow by the stove. "I could tell you it had to do with air pressure and the density of the blanket—or I could tell you it was magic."

"I'd rather think it was magic."

He issued a short, wry laugh. "And I'd rather think it was elementary physics."

"This, from the founder and chief executive of the Magic Shops."

"Magic doesn't exist."

"What a great logo for your stores. Maybe Neely, Henderson can build a campaign around it."

Rather than resent her gentle mocking, Judd seemed amused by it. "Don't you know why they're called magic *tricks?*" he said. "It's all about tricking people into rejecting reality and believing something that doesn't exist." He dipped his hand into the basin, then wiped it dry on his jeans. "You might think it's magic that the snow melted and we've got water to wash in. I think it's science."

"I think it's great," she said, trudging over to the basin. The thought of washing was heavenly.

Judd moved around the counter into the kitchen area and pulled a large bowl from a shelf. "Take out as much water as you need and use it at the sink." While she filled the bowl, he went to get his toiletries bag from his duffel. He gathered a bar of soap, a hairbrush and a tube of toothpaste. "Here," he said, handing them to her.

She stared at the proffered items. "You don't have to give me your things, Judd."

"Take them," he persisted, setting them on the counter by the dry sink when she didn't accept them from his hand. "Try not to get the bandage wet."

She felt oddly exposed, scrubbing her hands and face at the sink while he prowled around the cabin. Washing before bed wasn't the sort of thing one did in the presence of a stranger. She tried to convince herself that Judd wasn't a stranger—but he wasn't exactly a friend, either. In fact, she wasn't sure what he was.

A generous man, she decided, dabbing some of his toothpaste onto her finger and rubbing it onto her teeth. A circumspect but considerate man. Someone who kept to himself but couldn't prevent himself from nagging her not to get her bandage wet.

She remained with her back to him as she dried her hands and face on a paper towel and made her halting way over to her cot. After removing her loafers and sweater, she crawled under the cover.

"You shouldn't do that," Judd said.

"Hmm?"

"You shouldn't sleep in your clothes."

She sat up. He was standing as far from her as he could, his head angled, his gaze oblique. "I didn't happen to bring my jammies with me," she said. "Really, Judd, I'll be all right. It's just for one night."

He regarded her from his distance, then shook his head. "It's not good to sleep in clothes you've worn all day. I don't know how cold it's going to get in here overnight. If you sleep in your clothes you'll get chilled." He went to his duffel bag and pulled out a large gray sweatshirt. "Put this on," he said, walking toward her with his arm outstretched. "Let your clothing air out."

She opened her mouth to object. But when he dropped the sweatshirt into her lap, her voice failed her. The shirt was soft, so much softer and less constricting than what she had on.

"Are you sure you don't mind?"

"Of course I don't mind."

"It really isn't necessary. It's only one night . . ."

He strode to the door. "I'll be back in a few minutes," he said before exiting into the blustery night.

She ran her fingers over the fleecy gray fabric, then held it out in front of her. Some people showed what they were made of by talking, weeping, saying prayers, uncorking their feelings and letting them all spill out.

Some people showed what they were made of in other, less obvious ways.

Judd's generosity told Alana what he was made of.

She would wear his shirt tonight.

SOMEDAY I'LL SHOW THIS drawing to my children.

The dark timbre of her voice echoed inside his head. He wanted to think only of her drawing and the talent it revealed. But his mind kept abandoning the art for the artist. He thought about how she'd taken a dismal situation and extracted something aesthetic from it, just as she'd taken a stubby utility candle and turned it into a menorah. He thought about the mysterious shadows she'd thrown over his face and her own in the drawing, emphasizing the play of the candlelight on the table, on their hands.

She was like the candle. He was drawn to her light, her energy, her warmth and beauty. But candles burned, and they burned out. He had to get through the night without getting too close to her, without getting burned. Tomorrow they would be rescued. One night, and he would be safe.

He remained outdoors until his fingers and earlobes began to sting from the bitter cold, then reentered the cabin. Alana lay in a motionless mound under the blanket; all he could see of her was her long, dark hair strewn across the pillow. He sent her a silent thank-you for sparing him the sight of her in his sweatshirt, with those magnificent legs of hers on display.

His gratitude vanished when he turned to see her clothing folded across one of the chairs. Hanging from the ladder-back slats were a bra and panties, washed and dripping dry.

If they were there, they weren't on her. She was naked under his sweatshirt.

Of course a woman would want to wash out her lingerie. He couldn't blame her for that. If he didn't happen to have his duffel with him, packed with a week's worth of clothing, he might have been in a similar fix.

But still, the image of her naked body inside the plush folds of his shirt . . .

Swallowing, he groped in his duffel and pulled out an extra pair of cotton briefs. He stalked across the room and dropped them beside her pillow. "Put this on," he ordered.

She inched back the blanket and gazed up at him.

"Put it on." His tone brooked no argument.

Her eyes were too dark, too dazzling. He could scarcely withstand their power, let alone the knowledge that under his sweatshirt she was—

Don't think about it.

He returned to the duffel and pulled out the gray sweatpants that matched the shirt he'd lent her, along with a blue cotton T-shirt. He didn't own pajamas.

Closing his mind to every disturbing thought of her, he changed clothes in the kitchen area and washed. After adding a final log to the firebox, he went to blow out the candle, which was no more than a half-inch long.

"Don't," Alana called to him.

He straightened up and looked across the cabin.

She peeked out from under the blanket. "You're supposed to let it burn out on its own."

Some religious ritual, he presumed.

He lifted the lamp and used it to light his way to his cot. The lamp felt light; no doubt it had consumed the small quantity of kerosene he'd poured in. They were lucky the oil had lasted as long as it had.

Refusing to look at Alana's cot, he climbed into his own and twisted the knob until the wick went out.

He listened to Alana shifting and groaning as she sought a comfortable position. "How about some aspirin?" he asked. "Wasn't there some in that first aid kit?"

"I'm all right."

He'd never met a woman who resisted help more than she. "I could use a couple of aspirin, myself," he lied, figuring that would make her more willing to take the pills.

He walked back to his duffel, where he'd stashed the first aid kit when he'd finished cleaning the snow off the plane. The floorboards felt chilly beneath his bare feet; by morning the floor would be like ice. He located the bottle of aspirin, pretended to swallow a few, and then filled a cup with the water from the basin and carried it and two pills to her cot.

He sat on the edge of the mattress and handed her the cup. "I really don't need this," she whispered.

A silky lock of black hair fell across her cheek, and it took all his powers of restraint not to reach out and brush it back, not to trail his fingers over her smooth, soft skin one more time. "You do need this," he said, putting the aspirin in her hand. "It takes a while for the pain to start kicking in. You're just about due."

"Judd—"

"It's going to be a hell of a night for you if you don't take these."

She sighed and downed the pills. "You're incredibly bossy."

"You're incredibly stubborn."

She snuggled under the blanket and closed her eyes. "Good night," she muttered, making the words sound like an insult.

He laughed and returned to his own cot.

"You know what?" she called to him.

"What?"

"Some people think aspirin is just a chemical that works on your nervous system or something, but it's really magic."

He grinned. "Good night, Alana."

For a while the candle burned nobly on, casting a golden sheen no brighter than a night-light. Then it guttered and died, sending the room into darkness. The vents in the stove glowed orange but threw no light at all. The split logs snapped and spat as the fire consumed them.

Judd wondered if the wood would burn out as the candle had. There were only a couple of logs left beneath the overhang by the front door; he would have a hard time getting a fire going in the morning. He should have gathered some extra wood before retiring for the night.

His smile faded as he meditated on all the things he should have done: Collected the scattered wreckage of the plane into one area. Drunk enough whisky to numb his brain.

Booked a commercial flight to Boston—or rented a car and driven himself down.

Told Alana to keep her clothing on.

The fire hissed. The air was laden with the aroma of wood smoke. Although the mattress was thin, it wasn't uncomfortable.

He closed his eyes, stopped berating himself over everything he'd done wrong, and let fatigue have its way with him.

HER LAST THOUGHT before she fell asleep was that his shirt smelled of him.

Before she thought of that, she thought of him getting undressed by the stove. She had discreetly burrowed under the blanket, wriggling into the undershorts he'd given her and trying not to consider the provocative nature of what she was doing. Putting them on was simply a matter of expedience and comfort.

Not just her comfort but his.

Thinking about that forced her to consider the provocative nature of the situation once more. What she had on—or didn't have on—bothered him. And what he did or didn't have on bothered her.

They were adults. They had survived a plane crash; surely they could survive a night together in this cabin. At least *she* could, if she stopped thinking about how male the sweatshirt smelled, and about the sweatshirt's irresistibly male owner.

The warm solace of sleep spread through her. Her body's stiffness fell away. Her mind went blank, shedding every tempting, troubling thought of Judd Singer.

She dreamed of snow, billowing, drifting, stretching before her, draped pristinely among the trees. She dreamed of reaching toward it, stretching, yearning for it, pressing on. She dreamed of coming down with a lethal impact, pieces of the world wrenched from her. She was spinning, twisting, tearing—

Screaming.

"Alana."

In her dream she was being sucked into the funnel, and he was trying to pull her out, and she was screaming and screaming. His voice broke through her frenzy, murmuring her name over and over, trying to drag her back, away from the light, out of the funnel, back to life.

"Alana. Open your eyes."

She did. Judd's silhouette loomed above her, his arms gathering her to him, his voice a sweet murmur in the unfamiliar room.

"It's okay," he said. "It was just a dream."

She began to shake. She felt as if she were trapped in a torturous time loop, doomed to relive the crash again and again. She was mortified by how defenseless she felt, how terrified.

"I'm acting like a baby," she moaned, covering her face with her hands and feeling the tears seep through her fingers.

"No." He rocked her, stroked her hair, let her soak his T-shirt with her tears. "You lived through something awful. It's natural to be upset."

"I hate crying. I hate being weak. I hate this whole thing." That wasn't quite true, she acknowledged silently. She liked having Judd's arms around her, having his lean, hard chest to rest her head against. But then, she hated liking that as much as she did.

He continued to run his hand over her hair, skimming the back of her neck and smoothing the tangled tresses. "You aren't weak," he said. "If you *didn't* have a nightmare I'd be worried."

"You didn't have a nightmare."

His broad, firm chest absorbed her trembling. His arms remained circled firmly around her. "I wasn't the pilot," he said. "I didn't have another person's life in my hands. And I didn't get hurt."

"The dream hurts worse than anything else. Not the dream, but being so frightened. That's what hurts."

She felt him nod, felt his fingers twine through her hair again. It felt too good, too soothing. She couldn't let herself need him like this.

Sighing, she drew back. The air in the room had turned frigid. No longer cuddled within his warm embrace, she felt assaulted by the cold. Shivers racked her; her teeth chattered.

"You should have another blanket," he said, rising and heading back to his cot. He lifted his blanket and carried it to her.

"You can't give me yours. Aren't there any more blankets in the dresser?"

"I tied the only other blanket to the plane's wing."

"Well, you can't give me your blanket. You'll freeze to death if you do."

He stood above her, his blanket slung over his arm, a tall, lurking shadow in the chilly room. After a moment's hesitation, he shook the blanket out and spread it on top of hers, letting it float slowly, fluidly down onto her.

"No, Judd. I can't take it. You keep it."

Without a word, he went back to his cot, grabbed his pillow, and returned once more. He dropped his pillow next to hers, lifted the blankets and climbed in beside her. Then he pulled her quivering body into his strong arms, arranging her so her back nestled against his chest and his knees bent into the backs of hers.

She lay motionless, wondering how to tell him this was a bad idea. One of his arms worked its way under her pillow; the other curved over her waist. His thighs felt sleek and muscular through the fabric of his sweatpants. Her spine seemed much too eager to arch against his chest; her bottom fit much too snugly into the angle of his hips.

She took a deep breath and let it out. So what if he happened to be a blue-eyed Adonis? So what if he cared more for her well-being than anyone outside her family ever had? So what if he was willing to sacrifice a night's sleep—his own and hers—so they could stay warm in this desolate hovel?

So what if her entire body pulsed with awareness, if she felt less warm than hot in his protective embrace? He had no personal interest in her. Spending the night in her cot was an act of altruism on his part, nothing more.

At least she wasn't shivering anymore. She relaxed, growing accustomed to the virile body beside her. She didn't really want to go back to sleep, anyway. If she fell asleep she would find herself besieged by nightmares again.

She would just rest until morning. Just rest. Just close her eyes and empty her mind and rest.

HE WAS AWAKENED by his own arousal.

He was awakened by the tickly sensation of her silken hair brushing over his lips and chin. His lungs were filled with her scent and his arms were filled with her slumbering body, her head resting heavily on his shoulder, her bottom pressed up against him, her legs entwined with his.

He was hard and hungry, wrestling with the urge to move against her, to roll her onto her back and sink between her legs, to make her know exactly what he was feeling, to make her feel it just as strongly.

This was healthy. This was normal.

It was also completely out of line.

He forced himself to slide his arm out from under her and shift toward the edge of the cot. She rolled onto her back without his assistance, but she didn't wake up.

He propped himself on one arm and gazed down at her. Silver light spilled through the window and danced across her skin. For not the first time, he was stunned by the exotic length of her eyelashes, the fullness of her lips and the abundance of hair fanning out around her face in dense black waves. The loose neckline of his sweatshirt exposed her graceful throat, the hollow at its base and just enough of her left collarbone to reduce a man to sheer lust. It didn't help him to know that below her collarbones her breasts swelled full and lush, unrestrained by a bra.

His arousal increased.

He studied the gray-blue bruise under her left eye. He wanted to kiss it and make it better. He wanted to kiss her other bruises, the soft, smooth, wounded skin of her belly and hips. He wanted to imprint her with kisses the way the seat belt had imprinted her with welts, and then rise to kiss her breasts. The air in the cabin was ice cold, but she was womanly warmth, voluptuous heat, and he wanted her. He wanted her.

Suddenly she was awake, staring up at him.

Smothering a groan, he rolled away and got to his feet. Cripes, what was he thinking?

He knew damned well what he was thinking. The question was, did *she* know what he was thinking? Had she seen it in his eyes? Had she felt it in the tension of his body, the tautness of his flesh, the harshness of his breath? Did she know?

What the hell did she expect? When a healthy, normal man spent the night in a narrow cot with a beautiful woman, certain reflexes went into action. His response couldn't have shocked her. She wasn't a child.

Even so, he scrambled into his clothing as quickly as he could, his movements jerky, his fingers fumbling with the buttons, his breath visible in the cold interior of the cabin. Once he got a fire going in the stove, he would have a less hazardous way of warming himself up.

Remembering the nearly exhausted supply of firewood, he swore under his breath. He was freezing, he was hundreds of miles from the nearest cup of coffee, and he was going to have to tramp through the forest searching for enough wood to get a fire going. The ashes in the firebox were cold.

He dropped onto one of the chairs and shoved his feet into his boots. He took his various frustrations out on the laces, yanking and tying them with brutal aggression. Standing, he reached for his jacket and pulled it on. At the door he turned and checked on Alana.

She was watching him. The dark brilliance of her eyes conveyed that she understood exactly why he'd bolted from the cot—which only made it more imperative that he bolt from the cabin.

He did, literally hurling himself outside into the tart mountain morning. He scanned the area around the front door, saw no wood worth gathering, and glanced at the overhang, where he'd found the pile of split logs yesterday.

A stack of firewood stood there, a mound of kindling beside it.

Judd frowned. There couldn't have been more than a dozen logs in the pile yesterday. He was sure he'd used all but two or three of them. How could there be twenty logs there this morning?

He had been confused yesterday, that was how. More logs had been stacked under the overhang than he'd noticed. They'd been stacked in a way that had made it difficult to estimate the number. And he'd been dazed by the crash. He hadn't been thinking clearly.

Easy enough to explain.

After a quick trip to the outhouse, he gathered a few logs and an armful of kindling and reentered the cabin. Alana was leaning against one of the counters, fully clothed.

He moved directly to the stove. She watched him, the same quiet accusation in her eyes that he'd detected when he'd left the cabin. He tried to tune it out and focus on starting a fire. But he felt her gaze on him, appraising him, indicting him.

"You don't have to act like you're afraid of me, you know," she finally said.

"I'm not." It was at best a half truth. He wasn't afraid of her as much as himself, his impulses, his desires. Even when she was dressed he wanted her, far more than he should. He wanted her in his arms beneath those two toasty blankets. He wanted her legs woven through his and her breasts an inch from his hands, and the rounded flesh of her derriere rubbing against him.

He couldn't do anything about it, though. He wasn't looking for a love affair with Alana.

"I'm sorry if you felt awkward about the sleeping arrangement," she continued. Her willingness to keep the discussion alive in the face of his silence was another sign of how brave she was. "The fact is, once I was with you I didn't have any more nightmares. I don't know why, Judd, but it's true. Sleeping with you helped me."

Sleeping with you... Hearing her utter the words, even when he knew that sleeping was all they'd done, set his entire nervous system on edge. *Sleeping with you helped me.* Oh, hell, maybe if they had exploited the situation for all it was worth it would have helped them both.

He had to stop thinking that way. "I've got a girl-friend in New York," he said, desperate to establish a barrier between Alana and himself. As a rule, he considered Susan a woman he dated, not a girlfriend, but right now he needed to protect himself. He needed to draw an unbreachable line between himself and the dark-haired woman in the kitchen.

"New York—is that where you live?"

"Yes."

She opened a cabinet, closed it, opened another and closed it. "And you have a girlfriend there," she said, opening a third and studying its contents. "I'm very happy for you, Judd. You still don't have to be afraid of me."

"I'm not."

"Good. Because I'm really not a scary person."

Little did she know, she was the scariest person he'd ever met. Bold, beautiful and blunt—a frightening combination.

"I've got the fire going," he said, dusting off his hands on his thighs and standing. He lifted his eyes to Alana and saw something unexpected but no less welcome than the huge woodpile outside the cabin: she had a can of ground coffee in one hand and an old-fashioned stove-top percolator in the other.

Her triumphant smile lured a reluctant smile from him, too. With some caffeine in his system, he could cope with anything. Even Alana Halpern.

"Where did you find that?"

"Toward the back of this cabinet. Along with—" she pulled out a box of rolled oats "—this."

"Wow." The prospect of oatmeal had never excited him before. Now, it was manna from heaven.

"All we're missing is orange juice," she said, shuffling toward the basin with the percolator. "This is almost a regular breakfast."

Judd realized he was famished. Soup and crackers hadn't been much of a dinner. While Alana scooped coffee grounds into the percolator, he located a pot, measured some rolled oats and water into it, and set it on the stove to cook.

Ten minutes later they were seated at the table, devouring their oatmeal. Alana no longer seemed apprehensive about their helping themselves to the cabin's supplies. The way Judd felt, he'd gladly pay a premium for the hot, filling cereal. And the coffee. Especially the coffee.

"How are you feeling?" he asked, cupping his hands around his mug and inhaling the wonderful aroma.

"Okay."

"I should have a look at your cut."

She made a face. "You probably shouldn't. It's ghastly, isn't it?"

He shook his head. "It wasn't deep."

"I don't care about deep. I care about being scarred for life."

A slow grin tugged at his lips. Her vanity appealed to him. It made her more human. "I don't think you'll have a scar," he assured her.

He got the first aid kit and peeled the bandage from her forehead. Then he cleaned the gash and dressed it. That he could touch her without his nerves misfiring was a promising sign. He was tired of feeling overwhelmed by his yearning for her.

When he was done, Alana pushed herself to her feet and gathered the dishes.

"I'd like to go outside and check the plane," Judd said. "If you think you'll be all right—"

"Wait for me and I'll go with you."

"You should stay inside."

She glared at him. "And you should stop being a mother. I've already got one of those, and she can out-mother you, hands down."

"She's not here."

"Well, you make a lousy substitute. If you want to get out of doing the dishes, go ahead, go outside. I'll join you after I've cleaned up in here."

"There's nothing for you to do outside," he argued. "You'll just get cold."

She sent him another withering look, then carried the bowls to the dry sink.

She was truly the most obstinate woman he'd ever encountered. Yesterday, she could scarcely stand up by herself. She'd been unconscious. She'd moaned in pain every time she moved. She'd been assailed by nightmares. And now she was going to insist that she was well enough to go traipsing around in the bitter cold morning, her feet protected by nothing more substantial than a pair of leather loafers.

She was truly exasperating.

Damn, if it didn't turn him on even more.

The chilly mountain air would do him some good, he thought, donning his jacket, opening the door and stepping outside. The more time he spent in Alana's company, the more cooling off he needed.

Leaning forward into the frigid wind, he marched through the trees to the clearing. He stared at the battered, tattered fuselage, half covered with newly formed snowdrifts, and remembered how warm and womanly Alana had felt in bed, in his arms. An ice-filled gust chafed his cheeks and he thought about her legs, her soft flesh hidden by his sweatshirt. Swirling snowflakes snagged in his eyelashes and he recalled the velvet-wrapped steel of her voice saying, "You don't have to be afraid of me."

With a grim sigh, he conceded that even December in the snow-capped White Mountains of New Hampshire wasn't cold enough to freeze her out of his soul.

Chapter Five

She'd stay away from Judd Singer.

She'd spend the morning indoors, drawing, playing solitaire.

She could pretend that spending the night with him had left her unaffected, and that every time she glimpsed his knowing eyes she didn't feel them penetrate right to her soul. She could pretend she hadn't been aware of his hardness against the small of her back, the heat of his breath whispering through her hair. She could pretend she hadn't reacted just as powerfully to him as he had to her.

Sure. And while she was at it, she could pretend she'd spent last night at her parents' house in Brookline.

No, she couldn't stay indoors.

She resolutely reached for her jacket. Tying her scarf into a makeshift sling to hold her shoulder steady, she marched out of the cabin.

Judd's footprints cut a direct line toward the clearing. When she could, she stepped where his thick-soled boots had compressed the snow, so she wouldn't sink in and soak her shoes.

At the edge of the forest, she halted and surveyed the field. Chunks of the Beechcraft lay strewn before her. Except for the blanket on the right wing and the fresh dusting of snow the wind had spread over everything overnight, the scene looked much as it had when she'd last seen it.

She moved cautiously toward the dismembered landing gear near her, gripped one of the heavy steel struts and lugged it closer to the fuselage. Peering through the unbroken window in the passenger door, she found Judd seated inside, her headset resting in his lap. He jumped when she pulled open the door.

"What are you doing?" she asked.

"I'm trying to repair the headset so we can send out a transmission." He shifted in the seat, making room for her to join him inside the cockpit.

"Even if you do fix it, you'll need electrical power to get it to work."

"The engine has a battery, doesn't it?"

She gazed through the shattered windshield at the mangled nose of the plane. "It did. God knows if it survived the crash."

She watched as he wielded a screwdriver from the toolbox, meticulously disassembling the components of the headset. She focused on his fingers, thick but nimble, delicately gathering the tiny screws and storing them in his pocket so they wouldn't get lost. She'd been wearing that headset less than twenty-four hours ago, talking to a traffic controller at the Laconia airport.

The last person in civilization she'd spoken to, and he probably believed she was dead.

"It got pretty bent, didn't it?" she said.

Judd nodded.

"I'm lucky it didn't poke right through my skull."

"It couldn't. You're too hardheaded."

She tilted her head until she caught his eye. He sent her a grin. "Do you know what you're doing?" she asked as he began to separate the torn filaments of copper wire connected to the microphone.

"Yeah."

"You've done this sort of thing before?"

"It's basic electronics," he said, making her feel terribly ignorant.

She watched him work for a minute, then said, "I'm going to try to gather the debris into a central location. It may make us more visible."

He glanced up from the disconnected headset. "You shouldn't be lifting heavy stuff. Wait and I'll help you."

"I've got one good arm, Judd."

"And bruises all over you." His gaze flickered down toward her hips, then back up to her face. "Don't do anything with the wreckage. I'll take care of it."

That was all she needed to hear. "I'll do whatever the hell I want to do," she snapped, inching back to the door.

She spied her gloves on the cabin floor, next to a bloodied white handkerchief, and bent over to pick them up. Her sunglasses lay on the floor, too, cracked and twisted.

She realized how wise she'd been to take them off before the plane crashed. If she hadn't, they might have broken into her eyes.

Suppressing a shudder at the thought, she plucked her gloves off the floor and climbed out of the cockpit.

It dawned on her, only after she'd stalked around the fuselage on the trail of the severed wing, that she and Judd had been cramped together into the undamaged half of the cockpit, and during those few minutes, hovering just a scant several inches from him, she hadn't desired him one bit.

A sure sign that she was recovering.

SHE WAS LEANING against the side of the plane when he emerged from the cockpit a while later. He glanced at the mound of debris she'd accumulated near the intact right wing, then turned to her and frowned. Except for the red tip of her nose, she looked pale. She'd stopped using her scarf as a sling; it draped loosely around her neck, leaving her left arm to hang at her side. Her chest pumped beneath her jacket.

He looked more closely at the pile of rubber and scrap metal near the wing and cursed under his breath at the understanding that she'd made that pile.

"What's wrong with you?" he asked sharply.

"Nothing," she said, her voice carrying on a stream of white vapor. "I've been working hard, and now I'm taking a rest."

"I mean, what's wrong with your brain? Why did you do all this?"

She returned his scowl. "I'm the pilot. It's my job."

He shook his head and ambled around the heap of scrap. No sense arguing with her. She'd only dig her heels in and make him feel like a fool for caring about her well-being.

"Did you find the battery?" he asked.

"What was left of it. Which wasn't much."

He cursed again. How long had he spent repairing the headset, and now he had nothing to power it with.

Why hadn't they been rescued? He was sure he'd heard a helicopter in the vicinity late yesterday afternoon. Why hadn't any come this morning? What were they waiting for?

What was *Judd* waiting for? "I'm going to search for a road," he declared. He'd been thinking about it the entire time he was fixing the headset. If no one was going to come and save them, they were going to have to find their own way out of this mess.

Her eyes immediately widened, and she pushed away from the side of the fuselage and slid her arm back into her sling. "A road? What road?"

"There's got to be a road leading to the cabin. Or a hiking trail."

"Have you seen any sign of one?"

"No. But how else could all the stuff in the cabin have gotten there? Someone either drove it in or hauled it on their backs. There has to be some way out of here."

She continued to approach him, continued to gaze at him. He saw the eagerness burning in her eyes and felt a combination of satisfaction and despair. Satisfaction because she didn't think he was insane to suggest that a road or trail existed. Despair because he knew what she was going to say next: "I'll come with you."

He was so ready to hear it, he said "No" before she'd finished speaking.

"Well, you're not going to leave me here."

"You're right. I'm going to leave you in the cabin where you can stay warm and wait for me."

"Wait for you! You think I'm going to sit there like a helpless little lady and *wait for you?*"

Actually, that was pretty close to what he'd thought. He should have known better than to expect that she'd agree. "It could be a long hike—"

"We'll go together."

"No," he said firmly. "Listen to me, Alana. We could be twenty or thirty miles from a ranger's station or a paved road. You can't walk that far, not in your condition and not in those loafers of yours."

"You *can* walk that far?"

"Yes."

As round with excitement as her eyes were before, now they narrowed with what appeared to be resentment. "Let me get this straight, Judd: I've just spent the past hour dragging this junk—" she gestured toward the loose pieces of wreckage "—into a pile so we'll be visible to a rescue crew, and now you're going to walk away. What are you going to do if a chopper shows up and you're ten miles from here?"

"You'll be rescued," he explained, exerting himself not to let her sarcasm get to him. "And you'll tell them where I am."

"I won't know where you are. What if you get hurt along the way? You'll die of exposure before anyone can reach you."

"This isn't like climbing the north face of Mount Everest," Judd argued. "It's going to be a road. Let's face it, there's a cast-iron stove in that cabin. Somebody drove a truck up here at least once."

"Oh, great," she said caustically. "A road. A four-lane highway, maybe. You'll be able to hitch a ride. Too bad you missed the morning rush hour."

Once again he wrestled with his temper. Fighting with her wasn't going to do either of them any good. "Alana—"

"Either we go together, or we stay here together. We're not going to split up, Judd. That's a sure way for both of us to end up dead."

He scrutinized her, now only a couple of feet from him, her chest still rising and falling, her deep breaths sending puffs of white mist into the air. If he brought her along, she would slow him down. She would aggravate her injuries. He might have to turn around and carry her back to the cabin.

On the other hand, if he left her behind, she might head off in the opposite direction on her own, just to prove he couldn't boss her around. And if she went off on her own . . .

He couldn't bear to contemplate the possibilities.

She'd saved his life. He owed her.

"Here's the deal," he yielded. "Let's just look around for a trail. If we find one, then we'll decide which one of us will take it."

His willingness to compromise mollified her. Her eyes regained their fiery glow and she pulled her jacket's collar higher around her neck. "Lead on, Macduff."

He didn't know where to lead—and the fact that he had an audience to witness his false turns and wrong moves annoyed him. But then, Alana hadn't balked when she'd had to bring a crippled plane down out of the sky.

"Let's scope out the area surrounding the cabin," he suggested.

He tried not to think about her loafers as they left the clearing. He tried not to notice her uneven gait, her left arm once again held immobile in the sling.

He tried not to remember how vulnerable she'd been last night, when sleep had stripped away her intrepid facade. But it was impossible. He knew she was in pain, and he felt guilty for setting such a brisk pace through the woods.

He consoled himself with the thought that he would have felt worse leaving her behind.

At the front step of the cabin he halted and scanned the woods. Spotting no obvious path, he stalked slowly to the rear of the cabin, Alana at his heels. Once more he scanned the surrounding woods, searching for an opening, a passageway, any sign of an exit out of the forest.

"There," he murmured.

"Where?"

He started toward the pine tree. Nestled among other trees, it bore a faint red circle of paint on its trunk slightly below Judd's eye level.

"Oh, God!" Alana let out a whoop of joy so pure Judd was glad she was with him. She jogged ahead of him in a lopsided rhythm to the tree, then fell against it, wrapped her good arm around its wide, straight trunk and hugged it.

Judd suspected that she was using the moment to catch her breath. He tactfully didn't comment on her fatigue, but instead searched for another marked tree. "There."

He and Alana moved through the woods searching for another tree adorned with paint. "There!" she shouted, spotting the next red marking. Her voice broke into melodious laughter.

He didn't want her to get her hopes up. As he'd warned, this trail could go on for miles before they came upon anything remotely resembling civilization. But it was *something*—and it was carrying them away from the crash, away from their calamity. It was leading them back to life, and Judd felt Alana's sheer pleasure illuminate his soul.

THE SOUND WAS SO DISTANT, it probably would have gone unnoticed by most people. But Alana had been listening for it.

They had stalled out after only about twenty minutes—which couldn't have carried them far, given how sluggishly Alana was walking. In a sense, the dead end made her feel better about having forced her way onto this mission. Even though she'd slowed Judd down, he wouldn't have gotten any farther than this point if he'd hiked alone. He would only have reached the dead end sooner.

She sat on a fallen log, squinting into the forest in search of another tree with red paint on its bark. Her hip throbbed relentlessly; her feet ached, her cheeks burned and her lungs rasped with each breath. Judd circled the log again and again, combing the forest with his gaze. He started toward a tree and then backed off when he recognized the discoloration on the trunk was nothing more than dried orange sap. He started toward another tree and then cursed, realizing it was the tree they'd just come from.

"The trail can't end here," he said.

"Well, it does," she muttered sourly. "Someone probably painted a dozen false trails through the forest just to drive us bonkers."

"I'm sure there's another tree up ahead. Maybe a deer chewed off the bark where it was painted."

"I hope the beast choked to death," Alana grumbled, then grimaced. She couldn't believe she'd said such a nasty thing. If only she hadn't been given reason for optimism, she wouldn't be so agonizingly disappointed now.

"You wait here," Judd said. "I'll go a little farther—"

"You'll get lost."

"I'll stay within shouting distance."

"Judd." It was crazy, but she couldn't abide the thought of his leaving her. She couldn't abide it in the clearing and she couldn't abide it here. They needed to stick together. She recalled what she'd reported to the control tower at the airport in Laconia: "There's just the two of us." That was the way it had to be—the two of them, together as a team.

She opened her mouth to object to his forging ahead on his own, but grew still when she heard the sound of an approaching helicopter.

Judd heard it, too.

He exchanged a look with her, as if seeking confirmation that he hadn't simply imagined the sound. She nodded.

He grabbed her hand, hauled her off the log and started racing in the direction they'd come from. Alana tried to keep up but she couldn't. Her feet were nearly numb from the cold; her back hurt. Her lungs felt as if they were on fire.

"Hurry!" he ordered her, running faster.

She stumbled, grabbed a low branch to keep from falling and struggled against a momentary bout of dizziness.

The sound grew louder.

Judd turned his back to her, reached behind him, and heaved her up into piggyback position. She let out a startled cry, then clung to his shoulder as he hooked his arms around her legs and jogged through the forest, following the marked trees from red dot to red dot to red dot, striving to reach the clearing ahead of the helicopter.

She couldn't believe how fast he was moving with her weight on his back. He felt strong and solid beneath her as she slid her sore arm from the looped scarf and wrapped it around his left shoulder. She ducked her head, pressing her cheek to the smooth, leather surface of his jacket, and she thanked the winter chill for the fact that her thighs were too numb to feel his fingers molded around her flesh.

The cabin loomed into view but Judd didn't slow down. The helicopter sounded louder yet, approaching the clearing from the opposite direction. Impossible though it seemed, Judd accelerated his pace. The icy wind burned her cheeks and tore at her hair. She hung on to him as if separation would bring death. *There's just the two of us,* she thought.

And they were going to be saved.

At the clearing, Judd eased her down. Her legs wobbled beneath her, but she didn't care. "We're here!" she shouted to the crystalline sky. "We're here! Come and get us!"

Judd gazed skyward, too, his mouth spread in an astonishing smile that ignited his eyes and dimpled his cheeks and revealed his even white teeth. In the time that she had known him, the few smiles he'd bestowed upon her had been reserved. This smile held nothing back.

The helicopter finally broke into view over the crests of the trees bordering the eastern end of the clearing. Alana moved her arms in wide arcs. Judd climbed onto the intact wing of the Beechcraft, and from there onto the roof of the plane, his footing sure on the icy surface.

The helicopter glided west, almost directly above them. Judd waved. Alana swung her arms furiously. The helicopter continued westward, never stopping, never even slowing.

After a minute it vanished over the treetops at the opposite edge of the clearing.

Alana stared after it, too shocked to move. Judd shielded his eyes as he scouted the helicopter's progress from his vantage point atop the plane. The sound of its blades grew quieter and quieter, fading until the moan of the wind drowned out the last dying strains.

"It's coming back," Alana declared. She couldn't accept any other possibility.

"No."

"It's coming back. They saw us, and they're going to meet up with another helicopter and then they'll both come back and get us."

"No." Judd leaped down onto the wing and from there onto the ground. "They didn't see us." His voice sounded dead.

"How could they not see us?" Alana gazed at the massive heap of scrap metal and torn rubber she'd accumulated at the center of the clearing. "They'd have to be blind not to see us."

"If they saw us they would have let us know. Even if they were meeting up with another helicopter, they would have signaled us first."

"Maybe not. Maybe they saw the plane but not us. They know there's something here, but they didn't bother to send a signal because they didn't see any human beings. All they saw was the wreckage. They'll come back."

"No."

"Damn it, don't take my hope away!" Judd didn't deserve her wrath, but she was furious and he was handy. Her gloved hands furling into fists, she turned on him. "We're going to get rescued! We are! I'm not going to give up!"

She wasn't sure if she actually intended to hit him. Evidently he thought she was. He wrapped his fingers around her wrists and forced her arms down to her sides. She sagged against him, closing her eyes against the tears that welled up.

Releasing her wrists, he arched his arms gently around her. She felt the rhythm of his lungs heaving in and out and recalled his wild gallop to the clearing with her on his back. How could she lash out at him? He wanted to be rescued every bit as much as she did.

"Maybe another chopper will come along," he said, not sounding terribly convinced.

"Maybe." If he was going to be stoical about this, so was she.

"Why don't we go back to the cabin and have some lunch?"

"Lunch," she agreed wearily as she pulled away from Judd. She wasn't hungry, but she was cold and tired.

Judd looped his arm around her shoulders and they made their slow way back to the cabin. The fire in the stove was low but still burning, the room pleasantly warm. Alana pried off her wet shoes and stomped to the stove to dry her feet while Judd brought in a couple of split logs.

They stood side by side before the revived fire, thawing out. She stared at the air rippling with heat above the firebox and reminded herself that instead of rage and self-pity she ought to feel gratitude that at least she and Judd had shelter. More than shelter, they had food. With every passing minute, she realized, the amount of money they'd have to leave for the cabin's owner increased.

They ought to make that blind idiot of a helicopter pilot pay for the food, she thought sullenly. It was his fault they had to eat lunch here.

"I'll fix some soup," she offered, swallowing to keep her bitterness from rising up and spilling over.

"Okay."

Preparing lunch gave her a physical outlet for her anger. She banged the pot onto the counter, turned the knob on the can opener with vicious force, flung the soup into the pot and set it on the burner with a clatter. While it heated she opened and slammed cabinet doors, searching for crackers. Judd's tranquil preparation of a fresh pot of coffee irritated her.

"How can you be so calm?" she fumed, unable to bear his silence any longer.

He answered with an unreadable blue-eyed glance.

"I mean, really, you just don't let anything out. You're so damn quiet all the time. Why don't you say something?"

"If I had something to say, I'd say it."

She detected a subtle reproof in his words. She knew it would do her no good to antagonize him, but she was frustrated about being the only one who'd run out of patience. "Tell me you weren't disappointed that that chopper didn't see us."

"You know I was disappointed."

"Then why don't you yell and bang things, like me?"

He surprised her by laughing.

To her even greater surprise, she laughed as well, a glum, defeated laugh. "You must think I'm nuts," she said, placing two bowls on the table with an admirable lack of violence.

"I think you're—" he searched for the right word "—demonstrative."

"Right. I've just given a demonstration of someone who's nuts."

His grin wasn't as wholehearted as the dimpled smile he'd worn outside when they'd first heard the helicopter, but it was warm and forgiving. "You're not nuts."

"Thank you, Dr. Freud. I feel so much better now."

He carried two mugs to the table, then returned to the stove for the percolator. "How *do* you feel?" he asked seriously. "How's your forehead?"

"It's fine."

"The bruise under your eye looks better."

"Great." She didn't want to inventory her injuries any more than she wanted to discuss her mental health.

But Judd persisted. "How about your..." He gestured vaguely toward her pelvic area. "Those bruises."

After the intimacy of their sleeping arrangement, she wouldn't have expected him to be shy about mentioning any part of her anatomy. He'd seen all her bruises, touched them, caressed the flesh surrounding them. His allusion to them now reminded her of how she'd felt when he had, how she'd felt in his arms, how she'd felt when he'd lifted her onto his back and cupped her bottom in his hands.

She didn't want to be reminded. She didn't want to feel what she felt. He had a girlfriend, and if only that damned helicopter had spotted her and Judd, she would have been rescued from a lot more than this hovel in the woods.

"I'm all right," she said sharply. "So leave me alone."

He tendered an enigmatic smile.

She regretted her flare of temper. None of this—the crash, their current predicament, her troubling attraction to him—was his fault. "It's just...I don't like people making a fuss over me."

"Why not?"

She brought a box of crackers to the table and settled into a chair. Sitting across from her, Judd stirred his soup. "I've got two older brothers," she said. "I'm the only girl in the family, and the youngest, and ever since I was born everybody has always fussed over me. Even now they still try to protect me. When I told my parents I was going to be an artist, they wanted to support me financially so I wouldn't go hungry. When I went to Europe they wanted to send me packages of food and clothing. When I've got a sniffle, my mother wants to rush across the river to Cambridge with a caldron of soup and every decongestant on the market."

"You live in Cambridge?"

Of all the things she'd said, she hadn't expected him to zero in on that. "Yes. Why?"

He shrugged. "I thought you lived in Boston."

"I rent the top floor of an old house near Porter Square," she told him. "It's perfect for my artwork—decent light and lots of room to spread out in."

"Spread out?"

"Painting is my favorite medium. I like to work on large canvases. I use the living room for my studio. I more or less live in the bedroom."

"I see." He ate a cracker, contemplating her. "The work you do for Neeley, Henderson isn't painting, is it?"

"No. That's just commercial art. I don't want to have to support myself with my paintings. If someone wants to buy a canvas, fine, but I'm not in the business of selling them or accepting commissions or anything like that. My art—the *real* stuff—comes from me and it belongs to me. I do it for myself."

He absorbed her claim. "How about your flying? Is that something you do for yourself?"

She thought about the destroyed plane in the clearing, about the last few dreadful seconds she'd spent piloting it, about whether she would ever fly again, for herself or anyone else. She used to enjoy flying. She used to love the feeling of power and freedom that came with it, the sense of breaking loose from the earth's constraints, defying gravity, knowing that she'd mastered the sky.

She wondered if she would ever be able to take the stick again.

"How did your protective family feel about your getting a pilot's license?" he asked.

She smiled wryly. "I didn't tell them until it was too late. I learned to fly when I was living in Israel. They were seven thousand miles away—too far away to stop me."

"How long did you live in Israel?"

"Nearly two years."

"Why?"

Why? Because she'd been tired of France and Italy. Because she'd had enough of modeling for life-drawing classes and giving private English lessons to anyone rich enough to pay her. Because the summer she'd spent as an au pair in the south of France, her employer's husband had kept coming on to her until she'd had to quit. Because she had known that once she returned to the United States many years would pass before she'd have the opportunity to travel like that again.

"Because I'd always wanted to visit Israel," she said simply. "Because it was supposed to be my home-land."

He ruminated for a moment. "There's a name for that, isn't there?"

"You mean, moving to the homeland? It's called *aliyah*—but that wasn't why I went. *Aliyah* is a commitment to settle permanently in Israel, and become a citizen. I was only visiting."

"Two years is a long visit."

"I hadn't expected to stay that long." She nibbled on a cracker and reminisced. "I spent some time on a kibbutz. I explored the countryside and painted a lot of landscapes. Gorgeous desert scenes. The desert really does bloom there, and the light is incredible." She allowed herself a nostalgic smile. At long last, she could look back on her years in Israel without having the unhappy memories tarnish the happy ones. "Then I went to Haifa, and I got a job teaching an art class for the cousin of a friend from the kibbutz who had taken a maternity leave. So I wound up spending a lot longer in Israel than I'd originally intended.''

"Where did flying fit in?"

She regarded Judd thoughtfully. He had already told her he had a girlfriend; she supposed she could be honest with him, too. "I got to know a member of the Israeli Air Force. He taught me."

Judd looked intrigued, but also a little skeptical. "Air force planes are pretty sophisticated."

"I didn't fly the jet-fighters Ben was trained to fly. He taught me some of the simpler machines, though. He lived to fly. It was more than just his career—it was his life. And it was something I wanted to share with him."

Judd polished off his soup, his eyes never leaving Alana. "You wanted to share his life with him?"

"We were in love," she admitted. Two years ago her voice might have cracked when she talked about Benyamin Charetz, the dark, dashing fighter pilot who'd stolen her heart. A year ago, her eyes might have grown misty. But she'd recovered.

Judd continued to stare at her. His eyes held a question, one he was diplomatic enough not to ask.

She answered, anyway. "He married someone else."

"Why?" Judd blurted out, as if the very idea were preposterous.

She smiled at the implied compliment. "His parents wanted him to marry a Sabra—a native Israeli. He acceded to their wishes."

"I would have rebelled."

Another compliment. Alana refused to let herself take it personally. "You're a different kind of man."

She lifted her mug to her lips and took a sip of coffee. Judd was still watching her, his gaze unflinching, his eyes as endlessly blue as the sky Ben had taught her to conquer. A day's growth of beard shadowed Judd's jaw and his lips curved in a mysterious half smile.

The air seemed charged. She'd said too much, revealed too much, and she scrambled for something safe to talk about. "I wish we had some cocoa," she said, lowering her mug back to the table. "That's what you're supposed to drink after spending all morning outdoors in the snow."

His smile widened slightly. "Why don't we spend the afternoon indoors?"

In truth, she didn't really want to go back outside. She didn't want to loiter in the cold, waiting for the next helicopter to fly by.

"I found a deck of cards in the kitchen," she told him.

His smile grew even brighter. Not quite big enough to form dimples or set his eyes sparkling, but then, a deck of cards wasn't the same as a rescue helicopter. The only thing cards could save them from was cabin fever.

While she cleared the table, Judd went outside to get some more firewood. She rinsed the bowls in the basin, then carried it outside to fill with snow.

Judd was hunkered down next to the door, appraising the firewood stack. "How's our supply?" she asked.

"Good," he said, sounding perplexed.

"I'll bet there's an axe somewhere, if you think we might need more."

"We've got enough to last a while. It seems like…" He drifted off, frowning.

"It seems like what?"

He shook his head as if to clear it. "I don't know. I thought we'd used a lot more wood than we have."

"Hardwood burns slowly."

He shrugged, as if he didn't quite accept that explanation. "I guess." Standing, he took the empty basin from her. "You carry in the wood," he said, handing her two logs. "I'll fill this. It's pretty heavy when it's full."

She went back inside, added one log to the firebox and dropped the other on the floor beside the stove. Judd lugged the full basin in and set it on the stove with a thud.

Silence filled the cabin. She remembered the glorious sound of the helicopter's chugging motor, and a ripple of sadness pulsed through her. To stave it off, she pulled the deck of cards from the drawer. "Gin rummy?"

"Okay."

They dropped into the seats across from each other. She shuffled the cards. "Penny a point?"

His eyes tightened on her, and then he laughed. "Do you really want to play for money?"

"I intend to win."

"Then how about a dollar a point?"

She smiled confidently. "Mark Neeley would kill me if I won that much off you."

"Mighty sure of yourself, aren't you?"

"You bet I am." She dealt the cards and sorted her hand. Judd played the first card. "I should probably warn you, I was the gin rummy champion at the Rhode Island School of Design for two years running.''

He appeared unimpressed. "Did you play for a penny a point there?"

"No. I played for pride." She discarded a card and sent him a malevolent stare.

Ignoring her look, he picked a card and discarded. "Pride, huh?"

"I won a great deal of pride during my student days."

"That explains a lot." He picked up her discard, threw down a card and said, "Gin."

"Aargh!" She spread out her hand and tallied up the points. "I only let you win that round to lull you into a false sense of security."

"You didn't do it to give me pride?"

"I'm giving you twenty-three points. That's all you're getting from me."

He collected the cards and shuffled them with the flair of a Las Vegas blackjack dealer. It occurred to Alana that Judd might be a better card player than she'd realized. "Showing off, are we?"

"We are," he said succinctly, then spread the deck out in front of her. "Pick a card, any card."

She eyed him askance. "Is this a trick?"

"Pick a card and find out."

Still eyeing him dubiously, she lifted a card and studied it, her hand cupped carefully around it.

"Five of hearts," he guessed.

She gasped. "How did you do that?" she asked, throwing down the five of hearts.

He chuckled, scooped up the cards and shuffled them some more.

"Do it again," she demanded when he appeared ready to deal.

His eyes glinting dangerously, he cut the deck and spread the cards across the table. Sneaking furtive glances at him to see if she could catch him cheating, she selected a card, dragged it facedown to the end of the table and then lifted it up.

"Ace of diamonds," he said.

She cursed and tossed down the ace of diamonds, then burst into laughter. "Come on! Tell me!"

"Tell you what?"

"How you do that. Is it a trick you sell in your shops?"

He gathered up the cards and shuffled them. "I sell rigged decks in my shops, along with books of card tricks. But you know this isn't a rigged deck."

"Then how did you guess my card? Magic?"

His smile faded, growing almost wistful. "It's a trick. All magic is just tricks."

"Don't disillusion me."

"Then don't ask how I did it," he said, dealing out the cards.

She ignored the ten cards he'd given her. "Just tell me, yes or no, are you a magician?"

He avoided looking at her by sorting his cards. "I used to do magic shows. I haven't done them for years, though."

"Did you do magic besides card tricks?"

"It wasn't magic," he insisted. "It's just tricks. Sleight of hand. Fooling people. There's no such thing as magic."

"With an attitude like that, your shows must have been thrilling."

He shrugged. "They worked."

"Did you pull rabbits out of hats?"

Still smiling, he shook his head. "I did chemical tricks. Mr. Wizard stuff. Turning 'water' into 'wine.' Levitating Ping-Pong balls. Creating invisible ink."

"You performed a whole show of tricks like that?"

"It wasn't anything that formal," he said, then fell silent as he studied his cards.

Alana got the distinct impression that he was done discussing his history as a magician. But she was too intrigued to let the subject drop. "Where did you perform?"

He peered at her above his cards, then leaned back in his chair and lowered his cards to the table, resigned to her continued questions. "In class, at first."

"School?"

"It kept the kids off my back."

"Why would the kids be on your back?" she blurted out. Judd was so big and strong, she couldn't imagine anyone daring to pick on him. Unless he'd been a late bloomer, a skinny, scrawny youngster.

"I was . . ." He lifted his cards and pretended to examine them, but Alana suspected he was only biding his time, trying to figure out how—or even whether—to answer her. "I was different."

"You don't seem very different to me—unless kids in Idaho are different from kids everywhere else."

He picked at the corner of a card with his index finger. "I was a science whiz. An egghead, I guess."

"And the kids got on your back for that?"

He sighed. "Most of them didn't get on my back for that. There was one boy, though. A leader. A bully. He called me a dirty kike."

Alana gaped at Judd. She couldn't believe things like that still happened. They certainly didn't happen in Brookline or Cambridge or any other place she'd ever lived. "And you shut him up by staging a magic show?" she asked dubiously.

"I shut him up by beating the stuffing out of him in the schoolyard."

"Good."

"After that, some of the kids were afraid of me. They thought I was weird." He examined his cards intently. "My father got me interested in chemistry, and I started experimenting, doing tricks. The science teacher asked me to do the tricks in school, and I did. The kids still thought I was weird, but it gave them something to like about me."

"I'll bet you were very popular in high school."

He arched his eyebrows.

"You're good-looking and smart. You beat up a bully. That would have been worth a lot of points in my high school."

There was no humor in his smile. "Maybe I was popular, I don't know. But I didn't trust too many people. When Hank Felling called me a kike, not one of the other kids spoke up. Not one. Not even the kids I considered my friends. So..." He gave an eloquent shrug.

Alana continued to gaze at him. That he had told her something so personal moved her. She could begin to understand where he came from, who he was, how he'd wound up so reserved, so guarded.

She wanted to gather him into her arms and tell him the world was a kinder, more accepting place than he might have known in his youth. She restrained herself, though, and busied herself arranging her cards. "How did you go from doing chemistry magic in school to owning a chain of fancy toy shops?"

Judd drew a card. "I started doing my magic shows at birthday parties and county fairs. When I went to college I continued to do the show. I could make a decent dollar with it, and the money came in handy."

"Wait a minute," she interrupted. "I thought you said your father was a doctor."

"The lone doctor in a hardscrabble town. We were as poor as everybody else." He rearranged his cards, then threw off a jack. "After a while I got to hate doing the show. But lots of people wanted to learn my tricks. I printed up a booklet explaining the tricks, and started selling it. The thing snowballed from there."

"Lots of people want to be magicians, I guess."

"Lots of people want to believe in magic."

"Why don't you?"

He sighed. "It has nothing to do with what I want to believe. I know what it is—and there's nothing 'magic' about it."

"I picked a card out of the pile, and you knew what it was. Twice."

"Yeah."

"And that wasn't magic?"

He regarded her coolly. "I thought you didn't want to be disillusioned."

She set her jaw. "Disillusion me."

He hesitated for a moment, then said, "I saw the cards reflected in your eyes."

That he could see things in her eyes stunned her. If he could read a card face in her eyes, what else could he see? What secrets were reflected in them? What yearning?

"I don't believe you," she said, hearing something akin to panic in her voice. "How come I can't see your cards reflected in your eyes?"

"My eyes are too light. Your eyes are incredibly dark."

"I don't believe you," she repeated. She wasn't referring to her eyes—which, while dark, were as credible as anyone else's eyes. She was referring to his trick. She couldn't accept that it was as simple as he made it sound.

"Believe what you want," he invited her. He lifted his cards and discarded one onto the pile.

She watched him, wishing she could read the reflections in his eyes as easily as he read hers. He only studied his cards, refusing to meet her gaze.

Somewhere beyond the crackling of the fire in the stove, the crude wooden walls of the cabin, the singing of the wind in the trees, she heard the far-off chatter of a helicopter approaching. And she believed.

Chapter Six

Most mysteries had explanations, Judd knew. Like the mystery of Alana. He had wondered why she talked about her family, yet never mentioned a boyfriend. He'd been puzzled that such an enchanting woman could be unattached.

Now he understood: she'd had herself a great love and it had ended in heartbreak. Leave it to her to fall for a pilot in the Israeli Air Force. No "boy next door" for Alana, no college sweetheart or office fling. If she was going to love someone, it would have to be a romance as extraordinary as she was.

So she was single, evidently still recovering from her international affair. In truth, she'd sounded pretty well recovered—but she clearly hadn't found anyone special enough to take the place of her dashing Israeli lover.

One mystery solved. But other mysteries remained unexplained. Like why the trail of red-painted trees had ended so abruptly. Or why the pile of firewood outside the cabin never seemed to shrink. No matter how much wood Judd carried inside, there was al-

ways more wood waiting for him beneath the overhang.

And the helicopters. Why did they keep overlooking him and Alana? This one, like the first, flew
straight over the clearing. Why the hell couldn't its
crew see what was directly below them?

He stood in the twilit clearing, staring at the chopper as it retreated southward. He wanted to kick things
and curse. But Alana was already doing enough of
that for both of them.

He watched her as she gave vent to her rage, shaking her fists at the receding helicopter. Her hair
whipped around her face in the wind; the tip of her
nose grew pink. She looked ravishingly beautiful.

He paced the length of the plane's right wing, making sure the blanket was securely fastened. Then he
returned to Alana and caught her hand in midflail.
Still grumbling expletives under her breath, she let him
steer her back through the woods to the cabin. He
paused to grab a couple of split logs from the woodpile before they went inside.

"Let's have a drink," he suggested once he had shut
the door behind them.

Alana ignored him. "How could they miss us?
How? Twice! It isn't fair, Judd! Those jerks should be
lined up and shot! I wonder how much they get paid
to botch their jobs!"

He added one of the logs to the firebox, then removed his jacket and headed for the kitchen. He
pulled out two glasses and the bottle of whisky. Alana
hadn't said she didn't want any, so he poured a hefty
portion into each glass.

She hobbled across the room to the dresser, where Judd had left the kerosene lamp last night. "Where are the matches?" she muttered. "We ought to get this thing going."

"I doubt there's any oil left in it."

"I can think of one way to find out," she said, carrying it to the counter and accepting the box of matches from Judd. "I don't suppose we have any more candles."

He didn't suppose they did, either. He'd been a fool to let her have her little Hanukkah celebration last night—more accurately, he'd been a fool to think they would be rescued before they had to spend a second night in this shack. By burning their only candle last night, Alana had left them without an alternative to the lamp. Although she'd gotten the wick to ignite, Judd knew it wouldn't stay lit for long.

He rummaged through the cabinets, searching for something—he wasn't sure what. Food. Meat. If he had to eat soup and crackers again, he'd gag.

Toward the back of a shelf, he came upon the two-inch stub of another utility candle. Setting it on the counter, he continued his quest for something that might satisfy his gnawing hunger.

A minute elapsed. Then from the table, he heard Alana's voice, low and dulcet: "Blessed art Thou, oh Lord, our God, who has kept us alive for another day—no thanks to those idiot helicopter pilots. Thank You for keeping us safe even if it's cold and dark and we both want to go home more than You can imagine. Thank You for the miracle of fermentation, which has given us this whisky, which might help us to forget how ticked off we both are at the moment.''

Glancing over his shoulder, Judd saw her bowed over the candle, which stood burning in the center of the ashtray. ''Damn it, Alana—we need that candle!''

She sent him a challenging look.

''The oil lamp isn't going to last. There's a teardrop's worth of kerosene in it. Once it burns out, we'll need that candle for light.''

''Fine,'' she snapped. ''We've got it for light.''

''And what are we going to do when it's gone?''

''We'll sit in the dark,'' she said defiantly. The candle illuminated her face from below, gilding the exotic lines and angles of it. Her arresting beauty momentarily dazed him. Sitting in the dark with her might not be such a bad idea.

No, he thought grimly, *it would be a* terrible *idea.* It would only complicate matters. He had to stay focused on the simple objective of keeping them both alive until they were rescued—or until they found their way down from the mountain.

He slammed a glass of whisky on the table in front of her and took a drink from his own glass, hoping it would alleviate his anger and frustration. Alana took a long, bracing swallow of the stuff. With a slight shudder, she set down her glass. ''I don't suppose you rustled up anything appetizing for supper,'' she half asked.

''Soup.''

''Ugh. I'd kill for a hamburger right now.''

He gestured toward the gun rack on the wall. "It may come to that."

She shuddered again. "I'm not a hunter. As a matter of fact, I think hunting is disgusting. It's one thing to eat meat, it's another to turn killing animals into an entertainment."

"Don't knock hunting," he argued as he returned to the kitchen to raid the soup supply. "If it weren't for hunters, this cabin wouldn't be here."

Alana pulled a face, then sank into a chair and guzzled some more whisky. "Maybe I'll get drunk tonight."

"What a terrific idea." Acid etched his words.

"Well, what should I do? I'm miserable, I'm depressed, my whole body hurts and not one but two helicopters flew right by us. Can you think of something better to do than tie one on?"

"It's the second night of your holiday," he reminded her, thinking churlishly about the candle she'd wasted because of it. "Why don't you sing a Hanukkah song or something?"

"A Hanukkah song, huh?" She emptied her glass, lowered it to the table, and began to sing.

"O Hanukkah, O Hanukkah, come light the menorah."

Her hushed contralto wafted through the room like a delicate fragrance, soothing him as the liquor hadn't.

"And while we are dancing,
The candles are burning low.
One for each night, they shed a sweet light
To remind us of days long ago."

When she was finished, it was as if her gaze was entrapped by the flickering candle.

"How about a dance?" he asked.

She glanced at him in surprise. He was surprised, himself; he didn't much care for dancing. But it might cheer them both up. And even if it did complicate matters, he wanted her in his arms.

"Do you know how to do the hora?"

He shook his head.

She rose and extended her arms. "Come on, I'll teach you."

He set the pot of soup on the stove and took her hands. Her fingers were slim and cool, almost unforgivably feminine against the hard calluses of his palms.

"It's a circle dance," she said, denying him the opportunity to pull her closer. "Like this." She stepped to the side, then kicked her right foot forward and gave a little hop on her left. It buckled beneath her.

He pulled her close then, to keep her from falling. The muffled cry that escaped her tore at him. Stroking his hand through her hair, he supported her until she regained her balance. "I guess you're not quite up to the hora," he said.

"It hurts. Everything hurts." She moaned, clinging to him and hiding her face against his chest. "I'm not drunk, Judd. I wish I were, but I'm not."

"I know."

"I hate hurting like this."

"Let me get you over to the bed—"

"No." She clung tighter, her fingers arching and flexing against his ribs. "Just—just hold me a minute, okay? Hold me till it stops hurting."

He would have held her until the end of eternity if it would make her pain go away. Feeling the tension in her shoulders made him aware of how she must have been suffering all day without a whimper.

Slowly, calmly, he walked her to the table and eased her into a chair. He squatted down in front of her so she wouldn't have to strain her neck to see him. "Is it your hips?"

She dismissed his concern with a shake of her head. "I'm okay, really."

"How's your abdomen?" *The skin I touched*, he almost said. *The satiny skin, the soft, curved flesh.*

She closed her eyes and sighed. "I'm okay."

Realizing how much he wanted to touch her again, he straightened up and returned to the kitchen. "A little more whisky might take the edge off the pain."

"Yeah, or else I'll pass out."

After refilling their glasses, he served the soup and joined her at the table. She consumed a few spoonfuls of the hot minestrone. "We're lucky they've got a little variety. Eating soup twice a day is bad enough. If we had to eat chicken noodle soup twice a day..." She wrinkled her nose.

"We're lucky we've got anything at all."

"I wish you'd complain," she said, sipping some whisky. "It isn't fair that I have to do all the complaining for the both of us. You don't complain enough, Judd. That's your problem."

He grinned. He liked the way the liquor loosened her up. "Is that my problem?"

"That, and you play gin too well. How much do I owe you, anyway?"

"A hundred thirty-eight dollars and fifty-seven cents."

"Like hell."

He laughed. So did she. There was a desolate undertone to their laughter, but it was better than cursing and bickering.

They finished their soup, and Judd tried to pretend he wasn't still hungry. "You sit," he ordered her as he cleared the dishes.

She watched him heat some water on the stove and then carry it to the sink. "Even more than a hamburger," she said, "I'd kill for a piece of chocolate cake. Or chocolate chip cookies."

"Warm apple pie with cheddar cheese."

"A hot fudge sundae."

"A walnut brownie," he said resolutely, "with a scoop of vanilla ice cream and hot fudge on top."

"And real whipped cream." She blew out a long breath. "What are we, masochists? Let's talk about all the horrible stuff we're missing by being here. Liver and onions."

"Reality-based TV crime shows."

"Stupid letters to the editor in the *Boston Globe*."

"Slushy sidewalks."

"Rush hour traffic."

He rinsed the bowls, shook them out and left them on the edge of the sink to dry. Then he turned to her. Her eyes were wide and clear in spite of the liquor she'd consumed. Her lashes were as thick as mink, her irises as dark.

His gaze traveled to the door, then returned to her. "I'm going to take a short walk. I'll be back soon."

"I'm coming with you," she said swiftly, pushing herself to her feet and clinging to the table until her legs stopped wobbling.

"Come on, Alana—you've got to take it easy. You hiked all morning, you tried to do the hora, and you nearly collapsed."

"And now I'm going to take a short walk with you." She shuffled to the chair where she'd left her coat.

"Alana—"

"Either I come with you or I go on my own. Which will it be?"

He sighed. "Put on your coat."

SHE CIRCLED her gloved hands around his elbow and let him usher her through the trampled snow to the clearing. The night was still, the air crystalline. What little effect the whisky had had on her was neutralized by the cold forest night.

He accommodated her faltering gait, walking slowly. In fact, walking didn't hurt her nearly as much as that jump-step in the hora had.

"Do you do this every night?" she asked.

"When I can."

"I'll bet walking through the city isn't as pleasant as this."

"It's different," he allowed. When they broke through the trees the moon spilled its silver light down on them, reflecting off the snow and giving the clearing an ethereal radiance.

"It's beautiful," Alana whispered. Even the mangled wreckage of the plane was transformed into something aesthetic by the shimmering moonlight. "If I'd known this was what you were doing last night…"

"What did you think I was doing?"

She peered up at him. "Avoiding me."

He met her earnest gaze, his eyes a silvery blue in the unearthly light. Then he turned to stare across the snowy field. "My father and I used to take after-dinner walks all the time when I was a child," he said.

"Really?" After dinner in her childhood home, Alana's father used to bring the newspaper into the den, turn on the network news, and immerse himself in current events while she and her brothers were banished to their bedrooms to do their homework.

"We'd walk through the neighborhood," Judd said, "and he'd tell me about the latest thinking on tonsillectomies, or he'd explain trigonometric ratios to me."

"Wow. No wonder you were a whiz kid in school."

He smiled wryly. "Sometimes we discussed less lofty subjects. Like whether Willie Mays was better than Mickey Mantle. Or why girls made no sense."

"Girls make plenty of sense," Alana retorted.

Judd laughed.

"What was your father's opinion? Surely if he could explain trigonometry, he must have been able to explain girls."

"Trig was a cinch compared to girls."

"We're not that mysterious."

He turned her to face him. The moon washed over his features, transforming them into a sculpted mosaic of silver and shadow. A tentative smile curved his lips. "Maybe the mystery is that boys can understand just about anything, but they can never understand girls." He ran his thumb tenderly along her bruised cheekbone. She felt a slight ache at his touch. "This one's fading," he said.

"I'm fine, Judd."

He opened his mouth as if to argue, then thought better of it. She couldn't keep him from worrying about her; maybe he couldn't keep himself from worrying.

"We should go back," he said, turning toward the cabin. He took her hand and tucked it into the crook of his elbow once more.

Alana tried to picture a young Judd ambling with his father through his small Idaho hometown. She envisioned him with paler blond hair, his eyes just as blue, his smile as enigmatic. He would be shorter, of course, and he wouldn't have a stubble of beard, but he would be adorable.

He wasn't adorable now. He was strong and quiet, calming and steadying.

He was the mystery, not Alana. He was the one who could perform magic and say there was nothing magic about it.

If she'd had to be marooned on this snowy mountaintop with someone, she was glad it was Judd Singer.

THERE WAS NO NEED for discussion. Judd presented her with his sweatshirt and a clean pair of briefs, then left the cabin while she changed, laundered some underthings, and got into bed.

A minute later he reentered the cabin with a couple of logs, which he placed in the firebox. She listened to the sounds of him preparing for bed. He carried the lamp with him to the dresser, and she sent him what she hoped was an amiable smile.

He appeared bemused. "The lamp lasted," he said.

She eyed the burning wick and shrugged. "Maybe there was more oil in it than you realized. Or maybe it just burns slowly."

"I guess." He twisted the dial until the wick went out, then slid under the covers next to her. Lying on his side, he wedged one arm under her pillow and arched the other casually around her waist. "Comfortable?"

"Yes." She closed her eyes and let the warmth of his body seep into hers. It wasn't an erotic warmth, like what she'd felt that morning. Somehow, during the course of the day, she'd become friends with Judd Singer. Right now she and Judd were victims—or, more accurately, *victors*—of fate. They would share this night, this cot, their heat and strength through another bitter-cold night in the mountain wilderness.

It was nothing more than that.

Sleep descended quickly upon her, swaddling her mind in empty black. No dreams of flying, or falling or funnels. Just the barren peace of Judd's steady respiration, the heaviness of his arm slung across her waist, the firm cushion of his chest against her back.

Abruptly the black was pierced by a tiny round light. It moved, drifted, widened and slanted into a shaft. A spotlight.

She heard the *chip-chip-chip* of the rotors. *A searchlight,* she thought, running toward it, hurling herself into the light. "Here!" she shouted at the helicopter. "We're here! Get us!"

"Alana."

"No!" The searchlight passed over her. She darted in a zigzag after it, chasing it, forcing her way back into its brightness. "Don't go! We're here! Don't leave us!"

"Alana."

The light slid over her face and into the trees. Gasping for breath, she raced after it, pumping her arms, kicking her feet through the densely packed snow. "No!" she screamed. "No! Don't go! Don't go away!"

"Alana." Someone was shaking her shoulders. "Alana. Wake up."

Opening her eyes, she saw only the darkness of the cabin, the faint orange glow of the embers in the firebox, the pallid moonlight trickling through the evergreens and into the window. As her vision adjusted, she made out Judd's face above hers, his eyes half open and bleary, his sharp jawline obscured by a shadow of beard. His hands were clamped tightly around her shoulders as he stared down at her.

She swallowed as the truth dawned on her. "I'm sorry."

"It's all right," he said, his tone hoarse with drowsiness.

"It was a different dream," she said. "They were flying over us, and I kept trying to get them to stop—"

"It's all right." His hands relented slightly, his fingertips moving on her shoulders in a soothing massage.

"They just kept going." Tears trembled along her lashes, blurring her view of him. "They wouldn't stop," she moaned, unsure about whether she was talking about the helicopter in her nightmare or the nightmares themselves. "They wouldn't stop."

"Try to rest," he urged, sliding his thumbs to the base of her neck and rubbing the knotted muscles there.

"I don't know what's the matter with me." She'd never been weepy, and she couldn't recall ever experiencing nightmares before. A few tears skidded down her cheeks, adding to her humiliation. "I'm such a wimp, waking you up like this, falling apart—"

His mouth came down on hers, unexpected, hard, freezing her words in her throat. Just as suddenly he pulled back, but his eyes continued to bear down on her with the same fierce, silencing power. She heard the rasp of her own breath and his, the snap of wood burning in the stove, the sigh of the wind outside the cabin. She felt his heat churning the narrow space between them, his fingers clenching against her shoulders.

Slowly, he lowered his mouth to hers again.

His lips whispered gently over hers this time, coaxing and caressing, nipping and nibbling. His hands relaxed, one moving up into the tangled depths of her hair and the other gliding down her back, drawing her toward him. She wedged her hands between their bodies with the vague notion of stopping him, but the feel of his chest through the thin cotton of his shirt, the sleek muscles and broad ribs, the ferocious pounding of his heart against her palm only made her want to pull him closer.

His tongue skimmed her lower lip and she felt her body go weak, as if her bones had melted into honey. She opened her mouth and he conquered it with an aggressive thrust.

He rose higher onto her and she slid her hands upward to his shoulders, his neck. His kiss grew hungrier, more demanding. She matched his demands with her own, battling the lunges of his tongue with hers, raking her fingers over his bristle of beard and into the soft, tawny waves of hair at his temples. He rose higher yet, aligning his body above hers, bringing one hand forward to trace the underside of her breast through the sweatshirt. When he rocked his hardness against her belly, the sound that tore from her throat was half a cry of pain, half a moan of blissful submission.

He pulled his mouth from hers to kiss her cheeks, her brow, the lowered lids of her eyes, the tip of her nose. Then he returned to her mouth, tender now, gliding with delicacy over her inflamed lips, trailing his teeth with exquisite care over the swollen flesh of her lower lip.

Her hips arched upward of their own volition. She was hot, burning, wanting him in a dangerous way. She felt a shiver ripple down his back as he pressed into the crevice between her thighs. His mouth opened over hers again, urgent, giving and taking in a ruthless clash of tongues. His hips ground into hers once more, and she groaned, the soreness of her bruises superseded by other sensations, deeper needs.

With a broken sigh, he leaned back. She gazed up into his eyes, so brilliant, so blue in the cabin's gloom. They glittered with longing and fear and other emotions she couldn't begin to decipher.

As abruptly as he'd kissed her he withdrew, snatching his pillow and blanket and fleeing to the cot on the other side of the dresser. He sank into the mattress, spread the blanket over himself, stared at the ceiling. Said nothing.

Alana observed his motionless silhouette in the cot across the room. She listened to his uneven breath and to her own frenetic pulse. To call him back to her bed would be the biggest mistake in the world. Yet to spend the night apart from him seemed unendurable.

He was no more than six feet away from her. It might as well have been a million miles.

Chapter Seven

Meat.

He eyed the gun rack. He hadn't done any shooting since his teenage years, and then only at empty cans with Robbie Sanford's air rifle. But right now he needed protein. He needed to fill his stomach with something substantial and nourishing. He needed to satisfy at least one of his hungers.

He needed to let loose, blast away, pull the trigger. He needed to dominate, to prevail, to release all the pent-up energy inside him. It was building, pressing on him, testing the limits of his self-restraint. All night long, in that cold, narrow cot, he'd felt the tension increase. He had to let it out, fire a gun, eat meat. If he didn't . . .

He didn't want to think about what might happen.

He couldn't bear to look at her. She moved silently through the kitchen, preparing a pot of coffee, glancing away whenever her gaze accidentally collided with his. Her eyes were ringed with shadow, indicating that she'd had as restless a night as he.

He would have cursed her beauty, except that it no longer mattered to him. Even if she weren't uncommonly pretty he would desire her. Her strength and obstinacy and guts turned him on as profoundly as her long, glossy hair, her hollow cheeks, her lissome figure.

Shoot, he resolved, turning to the gun rack again. Discharge a weapon. Make a bang. It might bring relief. Guns were phallic, weren't they?

He had already been outside, visiting the outhouse and giving Alana a chance to dress in private. Before reentering the cabin, he'd discovered a neat stack of firewood under the overhang by the door. He had nearly erupted in rage at the sight. He should have been thrilled not to have to search the forest for wood, but it infuriated him. There was no explanation for it, no logic behind it.

He was in no mood to believe in magic.

While he built up the fire, she prepared the coffee. When she set the percolator on the burner, her arm brushed his. Through his flannel shirt and her sweater he sensed an electrifying charge. The muscles below his abdomen clutched.

It was small consolation that she seemed to feel as flustered as he did. She scampered back to the other side of the counter to fix the oatmeal, assiduously avoiding his gaze.

As soon as the coffee was ready, he poured a cup for himself, hoping the caffeine would improve his spirits. Carrying the mug over to the gun rack, he scrutinized the rifles hanging there. He hoped he would find some shells in the cabin.

"You can't be serious," she said when he pulled one of the shotguns from the rack.

He took a long sip of coffee, then set down his mug and examined the weapon. "I need meat," he muttered, sighting the gun, testing its heft. "We both do. Ever hear of protein deprivation?"

"You're going to shoot an animal?"

What did she think he was going to do, club an animal over the head with the polished wood barrel?

"A little animal?" she cried. "You're going to shoot a little furry defenseless creature?"

"I'll try to shoot a big, bald one with sharp teeth."

"It's winter," she pointed out. "All the animals are going to be in hibernation."

"Maybe I'll get lucky and bag an insomniac." He made sure she was busy at the stove, stirring the oatmeal, before he ventured into the kitchen area and began a search for ammunition. In a drawer containing a lethal knife collection he located a box of shells. He loaded the shotgun, stashed the rest of the shells in his shirt pocket and selected a sheathed knife from the collection.

"Dear God," Alana muttered under her breath. "You look like Rambo."

"Without the sweat."

"You're actually going to use that knife on something? Something alive? It's revolting."

"I need meat," he said, sounding like a caveman and not caring. What he most needed was to get the hell out of the cabin before he did something truly revolting, like throw the pot of oatmeal across the room. Or throw Alana across the bed and convince her to kiss him the way she'd kissed him last night, all soft sighs and sweet strokes of her tongue, her hands twisting through the hair behind his ears and her hips undulating beneath him, so tempting, so arousing...

He had to get away from her. Yanking his jacket on, he stormed to the door and out.

The chilly, overcast morning helped him to unwind. If he couldn't have a cold shower, a cold hike in a snowy forest was the next best thing.

Other than a light wind ruffling through the trees, the morning was tranquil. The snow crunched beneath his feet as he tramped into the woods, diligently noting various landmarks along the way: a granite boulder, a mouldering log, a tree stump. After a few minutes he paused to survey his surroundings. His ears burned from the cold; his breath emerged in cottony puffs.

No game. No prey. Not a single living, moving beast—other than himself.

She was right, of course. Anything worth shooting would either be in hibernation or winging its way south for the winter.

Sitting on the tree stump, he continued to scan the area around him. He propped the shotgun across his knees and watched for signs of life in the forest.

Nothing.

To ward off thoughts of Alana, he conjured an image of Susan. He pictured her in a tailored suit, with a V-neck silk blouse under it and a string of pearls around her throat. He visualized her hair, shoulder length and chestnut brown, her creamy skin and her easy laugh. She was the epitome of everything he lacked right now; she was sophisticated, cosmopolitan, utterly divorced from the crude pursuit of survival. To her, survival meant being able to flag down a cab during a rainstorm.

His relationship with Susan was so simple, so undemanding.

It was hypocritical to throw her up as a shield against Alana. He and Susan dated, but they had no commitments, no long-range plans. Susan wasn't looking for a permanent arrangement with Judd any more than he was looking for one with her.

He wasn't looking for anything with Alana, either, he reminded himself. Nothing other than a rescue helicopter. And a well-rounded meal.

He stood, stomped the loose snow off his boots and resumed his hike, mentally recording the spruce tree with the split trunk, the tumble of rocks along a shallow ravine, the dead birch leaning against a live pine. He leaned against the pine, too, breathing deeply, feeling the weight of the shotgun against his shoulder.

He saw a movement.

With painstaking slowness, he positioned the shotgun to fire and watched the cluster of evergreen bushes where he'd noticed a trembling among the branches. He waited.

The branches trembled again, and a rabbit emerged from the underbrush. Maybe it wasn't big and bald and fanged, but it was as far from Flopsy, Mopsy and Cotton-tail as a rabbit could get. It was fat and old; the tip of one ear was missing, as was the first joint of the left forepaw. A ragged scar stretched along its ribs. It hobbled more than hopped, snuffling the ground and halting, snuffling and halting. Judd told himself he'd be doing the poor soul a favor by putting it out of its misery.

Maybe that was just so much rationalization. But he was entering his third day without protein. If it came down to the rabbit's life or his own, the rabbit didn't have a chance.

He lined up the sights, aimed, held his breath and squeezed the trigger.

SHE HAD TOO MUCH ENERGY. Anxiety, really. She'd spent all night reliving Judd's kiss, the heady potency of his lips crushing down on hers, his body on top of hers, his hand cupping her breast. Hour after hour until the sun rose, she'd lain alone in bed thinking of him across the room from her, running away.

She had to admire a man who remained faithful to his sweetheart in New York even when he was stranded in a cabin with a woman who was obviously receptive to his overtures. But gentleman that he was, he'd pulled back from temptation in the nick of time.

And the very next morning, he'd pulled back even further, vanishing, racing off to slaughter an innocent animal.

He wanted meat? Fine. Let him eat meat. Alana would deal with her nervous energy in her own way.

She was going to turn this damned hovel into a home for as long as she had to live in it. If the helicopters passed over them again, it would be easier to survive her disappointment if the floor was swept and the windows sparkling, if she could warm the atmosphere as efficiently as the stove warmed the air.

Warmth was what the place needed. If Alana had figured out anything, it was that there was a right way and a wrong way to generate warmth, and kissing Judd was definitely not the right way.

LUCK, he told himself, refusing to let his success go to his head. Luck had brought an animal out of hibernation—an animal that had apparently wound up on the wrong end of a rumble, given its raggedy ear and truncated paw. Luck had supplied Judd with a shotgun he could use. It had directed his aim, timed his trigger finger, felled the rabbit.

The same luck that had the kerosene lamp provide light for a day longer than it should have. The same luck that had situated a cabin a short hike from where the plane had crashed.

The same luck that had enabled him and Alana to survive the crash in the first place.

He gathered the snow-packed flesh in his hands and carried it through the woods to the cabin. He felt better, now. In control. Anticipating the physical satisfaction of a hot, filling meal and nothing more.

An inviting wisp of smoke curled up from the stovepipe chimney that rose above the roof of the cabin. For some reason, he felt compelled to wipe his feet before he opened the door.

Alana spun around. She was standing by the far wall, a piece of paper in her hands. Behind her another piece had been fastened to the slats of wood. If Judd wasn't mistaken, palm trees were sketched across it.

Palm trees?

Frowning, he scanned the room. The floor was swept so clean it actually seemed several shades lighter than the brownish gray he remembered. Pine cones and branches thick with needles were arrayed along the windowsills. The pillow cases had been laundered and were spread to dry across the backs of chairs. A small collection of utility candles stood in a row on the counter.

For a dingy shack, the place looked...nice. Very nice.

His eyes returned to the drawing of palm trees, then another, decorating another wall, of a sailboat skimming a lake. And another of a frothy roll of surf.

He looked at Alana. Her hair was pulled back from her face and fastened with a rubber band. She had removed the bandage over her eye, exposing the red slash across her brow. Her face looked clean and dewy, as though she'd scrubbed it as thoroughly as she'd scrubbed everything else.

"You've been busy," he said.

She glanced at his booty, then quickly raised her eyes to his face. "So have you."

He walked into the kitchen and unloaded the meat into the dry sink. Alana approached apprehensively, her nose wrinkling as she peered at it. Then she shoved up her sleeves and carried some water to the sink. "I wish we had something to work with."

"What do you mean?" he asked as he hung the gun back on the rack and removed his jacket.

"Onions, seasonings, something to fry the meat in. I guess there's some fat on it..." She shrugged.

He scrutinized her from his station by the gun rack. She had come a long way from acting the indignant guardian of cute little woodland critters. But now it wasn't a critter anymore. It was food.

"Soup," she said, turning from the sink.

"No!"

She flinched and glanced his way. Evidently he looked appalled, because she laughed. "There's some vegetable soup. I can simmer the meat in it and turn it into a stew. Don't worry, it won't resemble soup when I'm done with it."

"Thank God."

Still laughing, she pulled a can from the cabinet and returned to the sink. Her amusement informed him that she was a lot more relaxed than she'd been that morning. So, he realized, was he.

He was also starving. After draping his jacket across the rocker, he went back to the kitchen in search of a snack.

"Pretzels!" she exclaimed when she saw the box he'd pulled from a cabinet. "They're salty. I can grind some up and roll the meat in it."

"Don't grind them all," he said, scooping a handful from the box and devouring them. "Did you have any lunch?"

"I ate a ton of oatmeal. I'm not hungry."

He studied her from behind, noting the dainty shape of her shoulders beneath her baggy sweater, the streamlined curves of her hips. He longed to ask her how she felt, but he knew she'd get angry.

"You took off the bandage," he finally remarked.

"It was itching," she said without turning.

"I think you should keep the cut covered."

She glanced at him then, a swift look of barely concealed annoyance. "I think I should let the air get to it."

"All right." He held up his hands in surrender. "Not another word."

"Good."

"Did you hear any helicopters?"

"One," she answered. "I decided not to run outside. The pile of debris and the blanket would have been more noticeable than me running around the clearing and waving my hands."

"They didn't stop," he surmised.

She confirmed his guess with a nod of her head.

"It's weird, don't you think?"

She looked speculative. "I wonder what it means."

"Do you think it means something?"

She opened her mouth, then shut it and shook her head again. "I don't know, Judd. I believe in God. I believe in miracles. But these choppers flying right by us without seeing us . . ." She sighed. "It's shaken my faith a little."

Her voice was straightforward, but her words conveyed a heavy emotional weight. More than ever, he wished he could give her a hug, reassure her, tell her that whatever she did, she mustn't give up. One of them had to have faith, and it sure as hell wasn't him.

But he couldn't hug her. Even though he needed reassurance as much as she did, he couldn't dare to touch her.

He ate some more pretzels. She took a few, smashed them into crumbs and coated the meat before arranging the pieces in a skillet. "We'll eat well tonight, at least," she said as she brought the skillet to the stove. Passing close to him, she let her eyes meet his. "I'm sorry about this morning."

His hand halfway to his mouth with a pretzel, he paused. What was she sorry about? Haunting him throughout a long, agonizing night? Looking so irresistible? Having such satiny skin, such fathomless brown eyes?

"I mean, hunting as a sport...it just doesn't seem right to me. But to kill something for food, well, it isn't like you did it for fun. I appreciate your doing the hard part, Judd. I..." Aware that she was rambling, she took a deep breath and let it out. "Thank you."

"I thought cooking was the hard part," he joked.

She sent him a shy smile, then set the skillet on the burner. Once again he longed to touch her, to tell her he appreciated everything she had done, everything she was. He wanted to close his arms around her, press his lips to the crown of her head and swear to her that what little faith he still had was due to her honesty and courage.

He deliberately took a step backward, maintaining a prudent distance between them. "Thank you for cleaning the cabin."

"It helps, doesn't it?"

He wandered over to the sketches she'd hung on the wall. The fourth one, which she'd left on the table when he came in, depicted a field of wildflowers. "These pictures are really pretty," he said, looking for a place to hang the last drawing.

She shrugged. "I thought they'd warm the room up a bit. Decorating it with warm weather scenery."

"They do warm it up." He hung the wildflower drawing above the dresser.

The meat in the pan began to sizzle. Its aroma filled him with a sense of well-being. The ambiance was cozy and congenial.

Judd considered leaving. He was feeling too close to Alana, too beguiled by her.

He couldn't bring himself to walk out on her again, though. Every time he glimpsed her cut brow, her uneven stance, the fragile hollows of her cheeks, he wanted to protect her. He wanted to make everything all better. He wanted to restore her shaken faith.

Unable to do that, he wanted to keep her company.

"What would you be doing right now if you were home?" she asked.

"Right now? I'd be at my desk, calculating stock."

"Stock? Investments, you mean?"

"Inventory. This is the biggest selling season for the Magic Shops," he explained. "The weeks before Christmas. In order to maximize the consumer purchasing, you've got to make sure you've got the stock on the shelves."

"What are your best sellers?" she asked.

If she had asked while piloting him to Boston, he would have assumed she was fishing for information to help Neeley, Henderson and he wouldn't have answered. But now it was just a conversational gambit. Neeley, Henderson seemed like another universe, something no longer relevant to his life.

"Wands," he said.

"Magic wands?"

"Yes."

"Why? Do people actually think you can wave them around and make things happen?"

"Yes."

"Maybe they're right. The power of positive thinking and all. It's like good luck tokens. If you believe they'll work, you'll unconsciously put yourself into a frame of mind so they *will* work. When I was a kid, I had this rabbit's foot..." Staring at the meat in the skillet, she fell silent.

"That rabbit was actually missing a paw—"

"I'd rather not know," she said quickly, then shot him a sheepish grin. "So, it's a busy season at the Magic Shops, huh?"

"The busiest."

"Have you got a huge staff?"

"A very small one in New York. Most of our staff is in the shops, dealing directly with the customers. We keep the bureaucracy to a minimum."

"And maximize your profits that way."

"We do well."

She snorted. "According to Mark Neeley, you're a brilliant entrepreneur. You're a major success. The profits are just rolling in."

"If the profits were rolling in, I wouldn't need any advertising."

"If you didn't have profits, you couldn't afford Neeley, Henderson." She pulled the skillet away from the heat and smiled at Judd again. "You don't act like a brilliant entrepreneur."

He pondered her observation. "Is that a compliment or an insult?"

"A compliment. When I think of brilliant entrepreneurs, I think of hard-hitting money grubbers with buffed nails and thousand-dollar suits. I don't think of people who would take a catastrophe like this as well as you have."

He thought he hadn't taken it well at all. He'd been alternately brusque and doting. He'd let himself be captivated by Alana, imposed himself on her, grown obsessive about her. Wanted her, feared her and wanted her again.

"I'm going to mix this with the vegetables from the soup," she told him, returning to the kitchen. "We can use the broth as a sauce. I'll thicken it with some crushed pretzels. But you know what I'd like to do first?"

He eyed her warily. "What?"

"This is going to sound crazy, Judd, but I'd like to take a bath. I was thinking, I could heat some water in the basin. I just . . . I'd love to wash my hair."

"I have shampoo you can use," he said gesturing toward the toiletries bag on the counter. "I'd like a bath, too. Let me fill the basin. We're going to need lots of hot water."

"And after we're all washed up, we'll have a delicious meal," she said, her smile as fresh and delicate as the wildflowers she'd sketched. "It'll be just like real life. Like civilization. Like we're real people."

He almost blurted out that they *were* real, more real than the folks in the thousand-dollar suits with whom he had to do business in the place she called civilization. More real than the customers using their overextended charge cards to buy magic wands in his shops. More real than the account executives of Neeley, Henderson who made their living by persuading people to buy things they didn't need.

Here, far from civilization, he and Alana had made a civilization of their own out of food, whisky and candlelight, trust and honesty. More honesty than he was used to getting. More trust than he was used to giving.

This was as real as it got.

Chapter Eight

Alana sat in the rocker facing the window, trying to tune out the sounds coming from the kitchen. Although Judd had chivalrously left the cabin during her quick, efficient sponge bath, he had refused to send her outside while he washed. "Your hair is wet," he pointed out. "You'll catch your death."

She supposed she could have taken shelter in the Beechcraft's cockpit—although with its shattered windows, she would still have been freezing. Or she could have waited in the outhouse...

Forget that.

At least he was on the far side of the counter. If she accidentally turned around and glimpsed him, she probably wouldn't see anything below his waist.

Even that would cause her problems, however. Last night she'd felt his chest through his T-shirt, felt the supple muscles and sinews of his body. She could imagine what he looked like; indeed, she had spent the better part of her sleepless night imagining precisely that. To have her vision confirm what her mind already knew would only make matters worse.

So she rocked, gazed out the window at the snowy scenery outside the cabin and pretended she wasn't aware of every splash, every whisper of his hands scrubbing his skin. She focused on the towering trees beyond the glass and ignored the scents of soap and steam and clean male warmth that blended with the pungent aroma of the simmering meat and the perfume of the pine branches with which she'd decorated the cabin.

"Alana?" He called softly, as if afraid to startle her.

She flinched anyway. "Yes?" she addressed the window.

"It's okay—you can turn around."

Taking a deep breath, she did—and discovered it *wasn't* okay. He had on his jeans, but his shirt hung open, exposing a narrow band of his chest from his throat to his belt. It was as lean as she'd pictured it, as strongly contoured. A sparse dusting of gold-tinged curls covered the skin.

She swallowed and focused on his face. His hair was dark with dampness, grooved with lines from his comb. His eyes were clear and direct. "Can I ask a favor?"

"Of course," she said, even though there was no "of course" about it.

"I haven't got a mirror. I'm not too good at shaving by feel. Could you give me a little guidance?"

"Of course," she said again, rising and crossing to the counter. If she remained on the opposite side, it might buffer her from the tantalizing sight of his exposed torso.

He pulled a travel-size can of shaving cream out of his toiletries case and sprayed a mound of white foam into his palm. Alana watched, mesmerized in spite of herself, as he smeared the cream across his face. Some clung comically to the tip of his nose, and she instinctively reached out and wiped it off.

His eyes flashed at the brief contact, and she hastily became engrossed in wiping her fingers on a paper towel. Not until she heard the scrape of his razor against his cheek did she dare to look back at him.

He had his eyes closed now. Perhaps that enabled him to concentrate on the feel of his face. He stretched his cheek smooth while he wielded the blade. It skimmed too high, nearly nicking the skin below his eye.

"Here," she said, taking the razor from him. No matter how disconcerted she was by him, she wasn't going to let him slice himself to ribbons.

Steeling herself, she moved around the counter. He watched her intently, warily. "Have you ever done this before?" he asked.

"I used to share a bathroom with my brothers," she told him, rinsing off the razor in the bowl of water Judd had poured. "I've seen it done enough times to have a pretty good idea of how to do it."

She pressed her fingertips to his temple and ran the blade smoothly down the hard line of his jaw. She refused to dwell on how soft his hair felt, how smooth and warm his skin was. She refused to react to the sigh of his breath against her upturned face.

He stood immobile, his eyes never leaving her, his breath never altering its rhythm. He rested one hand on the counter; the other hung at his side. His shirt fell open with a casual sexiness that would have unnerved her if she'd allowed herself a second to think about it.

One side done. She used her thumb under his chin to turn his head, then repeated the procedure on the other side and under his jaw. He cupped his hand over hers to guide it over his upper lip.

"There," she said in an oddly breathless tone. She set down the razor and with a wet paper towel washed away the streaks of shaving cream. Only when she was done did she realize he still had his hand around hers. His eyes bore down on her, blue and silver and relentless.

Without releasing her, he stroked his hand and hers along the surface of his cheeks. "It feels good," he said.

What felt good? Being freshly shaven? Or moving her hand over his skin?

She couldn't meet his piercing gaze. Yet looking down proved equally hazardous. She viewed the strong column of his neck, his thick collarbones, the dark blond hair curling down the center of his chest to his navel, to his low-slung jeans. Staring at the simple brass belt buckle above his fly sent a sudden, unwanted surge of arousal through her.

As if he could read her mind, he slid her hand to his lips and pressed a kiss to her palm.

She heard herself moan. This shouldn't be happening. He had a girlfriend. They shouldn't start something they couldn't finish. They shouldn't—

And then he was weaving his fingers into her dark, wet hair, angling her face to his, touching his mouth to hers.

She moaned again, unable to stop him. Unable to stop herself.

His kiss permeated her with sensation. His hands clenched in her hair as his tongue tangled with hers, drinking her in, simultaneously filling and draining her. When her legs weakened he pressed her against the counter and deepened the kiss, taking everything she had to give.

She reached for him, and her hands slid under the open flaps of his shirt. His skin was hot, his muscles flexing against her palms. The hair on his chest curled softly around her fingers as she worked her way up toward his shoulders.

He felt so good, so strong and hard and good.

And back in New York, his lover was wringing her hands, wondering whether he was dead.

"No," Alana groaned, turning her face to end the kiss.

He moved his hands deeper into her hair and guided her head down onto his shoulder. Last night he'd been the one decent enough to stop things; today she'd taken over as the minister of propriety. But someone had had to bring this to a halt.

She felt him struggle with his breath, felt him fight his adamant hold on her. After a while his arms relented and he drew back.

His eyes locked with hers for an instant, too brief for her to read them. But then, she couldn't read eyes. Judd was the magician, not Alana. No doubt he'd read everything he needed to know in her eyes: that she wanted him. That she was frightened by how much she wanted him.

He reached for his toiletries bag, found a bottle of after-shave, and splashed the spice-scented astringent on his cheeks. Then he turned away and buttoned his shirt.

Glancing down, she noticed her hands—the hands that had so adroitly shaved him—were trembling.

Anxious to keep busy, she went to the stove and moved the pot of rabbit stew closer to the heat. She stirred it, twirling the spoon slowly and deliberately until the shivering sensation left her limbs. Without a word, Judd dumped the shaving water down the sink, then carried the basin outside to refill.

What was usually a one-minute chore took him five minutes. When he came back in, carrying the snow-filled basin in his hands and a couple of logs tucked under one arm, he sent Alana a diffident smile.

She would have liked to smile back, but she wasn't in a particularly smiley mood. There were too many things she wanted but couldn't have: a pain-free body, a rescue from this mountain, a genuine Hanukkah celebration.

Judd Singer.

"Where did you find all the candles?" he asked, setting down the basin and eyeing the collection of candles she'd excavated during her morning house-cleaning.

If he was going to pretend nothing had happened between them just moments ago, she might as well pretend, too. "They were scattered around. Whoever owns this place must toss them aside when they've burned down to a certain size. We're lucky he didn't throw them out."

"Especially since there's no way that gas lamp is going to last another night."

"Light it anyway," she said, stirring the contents of the pot.

"Alana, the thing shouldn't have even lasted through yesterday."

She shrugged. "When it's ready to burn out, it will." She wondered when—if ever—her attraction to Judd was going to burn out.

"And meanwhile, you're going to waste another candle on Hanukkah."

"It's not a waste."

With a skeptical frown, he lit the lamp, then knelt in front of the cabinet where the whisky was kept. "Well, well." He straightened up, holding out a different bottle. "Brandy."

"Where did you find that?"

"Way at the back. I didn't see it before." He uncorked the bottle, sniffed its contents and grinned. "It smells good."

Alana extended her hand, and he brought the bottle to her. She inhaled the rich fragrance and splashed a bit into the stew. "It can't hurt," she said with a shrug.

Judd carried the brandy and two glasses to the table. Alana served the stew and lit the candle. "Blessed art Thou, oh Lord, our God," she prayed. "Thank You for this wonderful meal. Thank You for Judd's successful hunt and for the brandy. Thank You for letting us live to see another night of Hanukkah.''

Her gaze met Judd's above the candle. She wished she could interpret the strange silver light in his eyes. Regret? Longing? Respect? Resolve? If only she knew the tricks for reading another person's eyes as well as he did.

"Amen," she said.

"Amen," he echoed, lifting his glass and touching it to hers before he drank his brandy.

After two days of soup, oatmeal and crackers, Alana had trouble finishing her portion of stew. It tasted delicious, though, rich and abundantly flavorful. And the brandy slid in a potent stream through her body, spreading an intoxicating warmth through her flesh.

She would survive. In its own way Judd's kiss was a disaster, able to demolish her as well as the plane crash might have. But she had survived that, and she would survive this, too. She would live to see another night, and another, until she and Judd were saved.

They cleared the table together by the light of the gas lamp. They had some leftover stew, and Judd tied the lid securely to the pot with a length of rope before he brought it outside to store in the snow. "I don't want an animal to get into it," he said, explaining the rope.

Once the dishes were stacked to dry, Judd helped Alana on with her jacket, then put on his own. They left the cabin together for their evening stroll. The night was overcast, the air raw. A feisty breeze tugged at her scarf.

Things would be okay when they returned to the cabin, she assured herself. Their bellies were full for the first time since the crash. Judd could sleep in his cot; Alana would be all right on her own. She would dream of palm trees and wildflowers, not crashes and inept rescue missions. She would dream of anything but Judd.

Thick clouds obliterated the moon in the clearing. The Beechcraft wreckage looked ominously dark and indistinct. The wind howled above the snow-covered slopes.

Judd tilted his head, straining, hearing something through the gales of wind. A few seconds later, she heard it too: the *chip-chip-chip-chip* of an approaching helicopter.

The sound grew louder, and then a bright light pierced through the clouds to stab the earth. "Oh, God, please!" she begged the sky, the light, the helicopter's pilot. "Oh, Judd—maybe—"

He touched her mouth with his fingertips. "Don't get your hopes up," he warned, although even in the night's gloom she could see his eyes glowing with optimism.

The searchlight slid across the destroyed plane, hovered, slid across it again and then skimmed the snow until it struck Judd's face, illuminating it. He squinted and shielded his eyes; Alana swung her arms. "We're here!" she yelled. "We're here!"

The searchlight darted around the clearing once more, then slanted across the trees to the south. The helicopter vanished into the clouds.

Alana waited for an expected wave of grief to crash into her. She felt only numb.

Judd's arm tightened around her shoulders. He stared after the helicopter for an endless minute, then focused on the broken plane, the red plaid blanket slapping against the wing as the wind blustered through the clearing.

"Let's go back," he suggested quietly, turning from the wreckage and leading her through the woods to the cabin. They entered in silence, closed the door, removed their outerwear.

A sigh tore loose from the deepest part of her soul. Had they seen a helicopter, or had they dreamed it? Was anything real, or had they both suffered the same delusion simultaneously? What if they were descending together into madness?

What if they'd dreamed *everything*? What if they had both perished in the crash, and wound up in some sort of "Twilight Zone," imprisoned in this snowy mountain world forever, thinking they were alive when they really weren't?

"I swear I'm losing my mind," she murmured as Judd handed her his sweatshirt.

"No."

"You wouldn't believe the ideas running through my head right now."

"I would."

She curled her fingers around the shirt and risked a quick glance at him. He was scrutinizing her, his concern evident in the steady blue of his eyes and the grim set of his mouth. "I'm going to have nightmares tonight," she said.

"Because of the helicopter?"

"Because..." She heard a tremor in her voice and looked away. "Because of everything. Because I'm going crazy."

"You're not crazy. If you weren't upset, *that* would be crazy."

"You're not upset," she pointed out.

"Yes, I am."

"Then *be* upset, damn it! Don't make me go crazy by myself!"

"Alana." He crossed the room and took her in his arms. After token resistance, she sagged against him.

"I wish you'd curse," she mumbled into his chest. "I wish you'd scream and stamp your feet or something."

"I go crazy other ways," he explained, touching his lips to the crown of her head.

She stiffened, even as her body warmed to the promise of his kisses, his passion. She couldn't yield to that marvelous heat, the rushing desire. She had to resist it.

If kissing her was Judd's way of going crazy, she had to do whatever she could to keep him sane.

"I'm sleeping alone tonight," she declared, knowing she wouldn't sleep a wink.

He swept his hand through her hair, twining his fingers into the thick, dark locks. "If that's what you want," he said after a minute.

"What do you want?"

A dry laugh escaped him. "Don't ask."

Her heart began to pound. She didn't want to hear him say he wanted her. Yet to leave the words unspoken between them was worse. "I already did."

He sighed. "I want..." His arms tightened around her. "I want us to live."

She felt her edginess wane and her trust in him expand. His kiss had been a way of living, of proving to himself that they were still alive, still together, united as they fought off death. It had had nothing to do with sex or seduction.

"We'll live," she promised, even though she had no way of controlling their destiny. "We can do it, Judd."

He pulled back and sent her a bittersweet smile. "Maybe we can."

TWENTY MINUTES after they'd both gotten into their respective cots, neither of them was asleep. Judd felt every wrinkle of the sheet beneath him, the thinness of the single blanket on top of him. He heard every movement Alana made, every restless twist and turn.

Closing his eyes, he envisioned the helicopter with its search light that saw nothing. Damn, he couldn't just sit around waiting for the next disappointment. He was going to have to find that trail. Somewhere beyond the last painted tree there had to be another red circle. If he didn't find it, they'd never get out of here.

"I'm going back to the trail tomorrow," he said, his voice carrying over the constant moan of the wind outside the cabin.

"We checked the trail. It went nowhere."

"Someone owns this cabin. Someone has used it in the past. They got here somehow."

"Maybe they fell out of the sky, like we did," she said with a morose laugh.

"I'm not joking, Alana. I'm going back out to find the trail tomorrow."

"Fine. We'll do that."

He should have known she would want to accompany him.

If she did, he would wind up kissing her instead of searching for trail markings. He'd wind up taking everything he wanted from her, everything he needed. He couldn't let that happen.

"You'll stay here," he decided.

"Judd—"

"Listen to me, Alana. I'll go. You'll stay here and watch for a rescue crew. I'll travel faster if I'm alone."

"Either that or you'll die."

"Thanks for the vote of confidence."

She sighed. "It could be dangerous, Judd. You know that as well as I do. What if you hike thirty miles without reaching anything? You'll have to spend the night outside."

"I'll risk it. Those damn helicopters aren't going to save us."

"So why should I stay here by myself?"

"Just in case they do come to save us."

He heard her shift again. Glancing toward her, he saw the silhouette of her curled into a ball for warmth. "What would I do if you didn't come back?"

She'd put into words his greatest fear. "I'll come back."

"If something happened to you—"

"Nothing's going to happen."

She moved again, punching her pillow. He heard her exhale heavily. "I can't do this."

"Do what?"

"Sleep. I'm freezing. I can't get comfortable. I don't know what's wrong with me, Judd, I . . ." She sat up, hunched over and rested her head in her hands.

Judd knew what was wrong with her. The same thing was wrong with him. He needed to hold her, and she needed to be held.

He swung out of bed, grabbed his blanket and pillow and crossed the room to her. She glanced up at him, her chin still propped up in her hands. "I'm not looking for anything romantic, Judd. I mean, that kiss—"

"I know." He dropped his pillow next to hers.

"There's your girlfriend, and—"

"I won't kiss you." That would be a difficult promise to keep—perhaps even more difficult than his promise not to let anything happen to him on the trail tomorrow. But he would keep it for her.

He stretched out beside her, drawing her down to the mattress and arranging her body along his, her back against his chest and her bottom cuddled into his hips. He felt painfully aware of the curve of her spine, the length of her legs, the delicate angles of her back.

He was too close to her, yet not nearly as close as he wanted to be. He found himself wondering whether sleeping with her was an act of noble sacrifice or quite simply the stupidest thing he'd ever done.

She nestled her head into the pillow beside him and sighed. Her hair smelled of his shampoo, a tart, subtle fragrance. He tried not to notice. Her back arched as she adjusted her shoulders. He held his breath and prayed for his body to remain unaffected by her innocent movement.

Her respiration grew deeper, more regular. He realized that she'd fallen asleep. Closing his eyes, he slid his arms around her, nuzzled her hair, paralleled her legs with his. Tomorrow he would leave her. He would pursue the red-paint trail away from this icy hell and save them both. He would hike out of her life, and when he next saw her it would be in a utility vehicle, accompanied by a park ranger and a paramedic and an inspector from the Civil Aeronautics Board.

And then they would go back to what they'd been, and they would stop mattering so much to each other. The past few nights would dissolve into nothing more than a bizarre memory.

That was what he wanted, he swore as he pulled Alana more snugly against himself. To live. That was all he wanted.

HE WOKE UP to a moaning sound. Opening his eyes, he stared for several seconds into the eerie white light infiltrating the room. He raised himself slowly so as not to jostle Alana, and peeked over her shoulder. She was asleep.

He heard the moan again. It came from outside. Turning, he saw that the window next to the bed was rattling, heaped with white.

He cursed.

Alana blinked and peered up at him. "What?" she asked groggily.

Her voice was so deliciously thick with sleep, he wanted nothing more than to huddle under the blankets with her. But the window rattled again, drawing his attention.

She stared at the window, too. "What is that? Snow?"

"I think so." He got out of bed, wincing when his bare feet hit the chilly floorboards, and strode to the window. A huge snowdrift piled up against the side of the cabin, reaching above the top of the window frame. The wind moaned again, a ghostly lament through the forest.

Alana pulled herself up to sit and shoved a heavy lock of hair out of her face. "Is it just a windstorm?"

"I don't know." He stalked across the room to the door and opened it. The wind hurled it back, nearly tearing it off its hinges and blasting a biting spray of snow and ice into his face. It took all his strength to force the door shut. "It's a blizzard."

"Oh, God." Alana propped her head in her hands and groaned. "They'll never send choppers out in a blizzard."

Nor would Judd find the trail down from the mountain. As long as the storm raged, they were trapped. "I've got to get a fire going," he said, trying not to shiver as he scrambled into warmer clothes. He tossed her clothing onto the cot so she could get dressed under the covers, then threw on his jacket and forged out into the storm to get some wood.

The woodpile was partly buried beneath the driving snow. The wind tore at his jacket and chapped his skin. Merely collecting an armful of wood and the pot of leftover stew left his hair caked with snow.

When he got back inside he was shivering. The logs tumbled out of his arms as he heaved against the door, straining to close it.

Alana hurried across the room to help him. "Was all this wood out there?"

"Yeah," he said, brushing the snow from his hair and shoulders, then shrugging out of his jacket. "Let's get a fire going."

They worked together, Alana breaking the kindling while Judd crumpled sheets of paper into the firebox. Once the fire was blazing, Alana stepped into her loafers and reached for her jacket. "Where are you going?" he asked.

"To the outhouse."

"I'll come with you," he said, donning his jacket once more. They ventured out into the storm.

Snow gusted horizontally, at strange angles, in whirlwind spirals. The stuff on the ground was knee deep on Judd, higher on Alana, and the drifts brought it higher yet. Each step down the narrow path was a struggle. They couldn't speak, couldn't even look straight ahead. They had to keep their heads bowed so the snow wouldn't fly into their eyes.

Judd huddled against the outhouse while Alana made use of it; then she waited while he went in. When he came back out, she was clinging to the side wall, her back layered with snow. Once again Judd wrapped an arm securely around her. He couldn't shake the feeling that if he let go of her on the path she would blow into a drift and be lost forever.

By the time they'd reached the safety of the cabin once more, they were gasping for breath. Judd collected a fresh armful of wood and left it in a heap beside the stove while Alana fixed a pot of coffee. Before filling the two mugs she poured a shot of whisky into each one.

Not until they had peeled off their jackets, dried their faces and hair and settled at the table with their coffee did either of them speak. "Where does the wood come from?" Alana asked.

"Outside the door," he told her, bemused by the question. She'd seen the woodpile herself.

"I mean, where does the pile outside the door come from?" she clarified. "We never seem to use it up."

He had no answer for her. The woodpile had perplexed him for days. Too difficult to contend with, he'd chosen to put it out of his mind.

Alana was putting it back into his mind. "What do you think?" he asked.

She cupped her hands around her mug and gazed across the table at him. The room was darker than it had been the past few days; the storm obliterated the sun, and the snowdrifts blocked the windows, keeping what little morning light there was from entering. "Magic?" she suggested.

"There's no such thing as magic," he argued. "I've told you that. Magic is just tricks."

"Do you think the woodpile is some sort of a trick?"

He shook his head, wishing they didn't have to have this discussion.

Alana wouldn't let it go. "Do you think it's luck?"

"If we had any luck, we would have been rescued days ago."

Lowering her gaze, she traced the rim of her mug with her index finger. "I think it's God."

"Get real."

"I am getting real."

A slow rage began to burn inside him. "You think God is leaving us the firewood?"

She raised her eyes to him again. They were as dark as night, as infinite, as alive with mystery. "You know the story of Hanukkah, don't you?"

Cripes. He didn't need this now. "Yes," he said brusquely, hoping to cut her off.

"The Syrians had taken over Jerusalem and tried to eradicate Judaism," she said, "and the Jews fled to the mountains. And then Judah led the Maccabees in a successful guerrilla campaign and won Jerusalem back."

"Right." His fuse was burning shorter. He could sense where she was headed, and he wanted to run the opposite way.

His curt response failed to deter her. "The Jews found their temple desecrated. They had to rebuild it and dedicate it. And they lit candles that burned for eight days. Just like our firewood is burning day after day, and the kerosene lamp—"

"The part about their finding one day's worth of oil that wound up lasting for eight days—there's no truth in it. The history doesn't bear it out. It never happened.''

"Miracles aren't about history," Alana pointed out. "They're about faith." She gestured toward the small collection of candles on the counter, the lamp that never seemed to run out of fuel, the firewood from the pile that kept replenishing itself. "Hanukkah is called the Festival of Lights, but it's really about survival. The Jews were attacked, they were routed from their homes and killed. Some concealed their identity, some went into hiding. Eventually they fought back. Even though they were outnumbered, they won. They survived. *That* was a miracle."

"So, what are you saying? That our survival is a miracle, and the wood is a miracle? That we're living out our own little Hanukkah pageant here?"

She traced the rim of her mug once more, her eyes glowing as she waited for his response.

He wanted to laugh, but it came out as a choked, bitter sound. "I don't believe any of that stuff," he said. "I can accept the history, but not the miracles. There were no miracles. The Jews fought and they won. It's not the first time an underdog triumphed over greater forces. Miracles have nothing to do with it."

"You haven't got a better explanation for the wood."

"At least I'm not going to accept a worse explanation." He drummed his fingers against the table, anxious to make her see reason. "I did magic shows. I know how they work. There's no such thing as magic.

It's all tricks. Illusions. Getting people to believe what they want to believe."

"Maybe I want to believe this is a miracle, then."

"It's a lousy miracle."

"Why?"

"Because if it's true, we're going to be stuck here for eight days."

"Maybe that's why the helicopters keep missing us."

Letting loose with a few pungent oaths, he stormed into the kitchen and filled a pot with water and rolled oats. Alana rose and followed him to the stove. "Look around, Judd. What do your eyes tell you?"

"They tell me," he retorted, "that we're trapped in a blizzard, and you've got a big cut on your forehead, and a lot of incompetent helicopter pilots have missed us. They tell me that we almost died and we still might die. If God's behind all this, I think He's really blown it. Okay?"

"Judd."

He waved a cooking spoon furiously at her. "Don't lecture me, Alana. You want to believe this is a miracle? Fine. Believe it's a miracle. I believe it was your skill as a pilot that saved our lives, and my shooting that got us meat, not a miracle."

"Then what about the firewood? And the candles? And the oil lamp? We should have used up the kerosene by now, but it's lasted all this time."

"Great. Swell." He gave free rein to his temper. "Maybe it'll last another few days. But if God were going to give me a miracle, I'd just as soon He got me the hell out of here." He stirred the oatmeal with absurd force, slopping water out of the pot. It splashed across the stove top with a hiss. "This isn't a game, Alana. It isn't make-believe. There's a killer blizzard going on out there. You want to burn an oil lamp for eight days? Be my guest—but keep me out of it."

Unperturbed, she refilled their cups with coffee. "You're already in it, Judd."

Damn it, there had to be a logical explanation for the oil lamp. Maybe he'd poured a greater quantity of kerosene into the well than he'd realized that first day. And the never-ending woodpile? He wasn't counting the logs properly. Or they were rolling down the hill from somewhere else, careening off trees and rocks and somehow coming to rest beneath the overhang. Or there was a shack not far away which Judd had somehow overlooked, and a hermit lived in it, and he was secretly supplying them with wood.

Any explanation would do, as long as it wasn't a miracle. Because if it *was* then he would have to believe the rest—that his imprisonment in this cold, isolated cabin was some sort of abysmal eight-day ritual.

That God was toying with them.

"I'm sick of oatmeal," he grumbled, spooning the porridge into two bowls and slamming them onto the table.

Alana presented him with a tolerant smile. "I don't blame you for being upset."

"I'm not upset!"

"If you could just have a little faith—"

"But I don't. All right?"

He dug into his oatmeal, feeling her eyes upon him. Perhaps his attitude was eating away at her faith. Perhaps he ought to play along, pretend he believed that everything was going to be all right and that God had a marvelous design laid out for their future. But too much honesty had passed between him and Alana to pretend now.

He felt her hand against his, sliding over his knuckles, cool and silky. He glanced up in surprise. After he'd promised not to kiss her, he wondered why she was initiating contact now, when he was at his meanest.

"I'll have faith for both of us," she said.

He gazed across the table at her. Her eyes communicated more than faith, more than concern about his bitter mood. As clearly as he'd seen the five of hearts and the ace of diamonds in them a few days ago, he saw a quiet, desperate need in them now.

He needed her, too. Today, when his hope was at its lowest ebb, he needed her more than ever.

He rotated his hand so their palms faced, and threaded his fingers through hers. Without another word they ate their cereal.

Outside, the wind continued to howl, the snow to fly. Inside, Judd held on to Alana. Right now, she was the only miracle he had.

Chapter Nine

"That's better," Alana said, jamming the extra sheet along the bottom of the door. The blizzard continued to rage around them, but she and Judd had managed to find most of the cabin's drafty cracks and patch them with paper toweling, the unused sheets in the dresser and, in the case of one window, the flannel shirt Judd had worn the day of the crash.

Even with their makeshift insulation, the cabin wasn't as warm as it had been just a day ago. Judd had brought every last piece of firewood inside, and he was parceling it out carefully, trying not to run through it before the storm let up.

"I can give you an extra sweater if you're still cold," he said, tucking the sleeves of his flannel shirt along the sides of the windowpane.

"No, I'm all right." She and Judd had eaten some of the leftover rabbit stew for lunch. It helped to keep her warm.

He surveyed the room one last time. "Would you like me to move the cot in front of the stove?"

"That's a good idea. Here, let me help you," she said, starting toward the cot. He waved her away and pushed the creaky metal-framed bed over by himself.

He seemed to be trying to make up for his show of foul temper that morning. He'd grown reflective after his outburst, not quite defeated but pensive, somber, slow to smile. Maybe that was why the room seemed colder than before.

She sat on the cot once he'd positioned it in front of the stove, and basked in the heat radiating from the firebox, which spilled amber light into the oddly twilit room. "Come," she said, patting the mattress next to her. "Talk to me. Tell me what I can do to cheer you up."

That provoked a tentative smile from him. "I'm okay," he drawled, although he accepted the invitation to join her on the cot. He stretched out on his side, propping his head in his hand and offering his thighs as a backrest for her.

"We could play cards," she suggested.

He shrugged, obviously not interested.

She crossed her legs and rested her elbows on her knees. "I could sing holiday songs," she offered. "You ain't heard nothing until you've heard me do 'Rock of Ages.'"

"'Rock of Ages'? I thought that was a Christian hymn."

"They have their version. We have ours." In a low voice, she began to sing: "Rock of Ages, let our song praise Thy saving power..."

Judd lifted his hand to her hair and twirled his fingers through the waving strands. "Why is Hanukkah such a big deal for you?" he asked.

She stopped singing and eyed him curiously. "Maybe I should ask why it's *not* a big deal for you."

He shrugged again. "I'm not religious."

"I'm not exactly Orthodox, myself. But the culture, Judd...Hanukkah is about our culture. It's what our ancestors did. The rituals pass from generation to generation. My grandparents celebrated Hanukkah, and their grandparents celebrated Hanukkah, and *their* grandparents did. And *your* grandparents celebrated it, too, I'll bet."

"I'm sure they did," he said quietly.

"Don't you want that connection to them? Don't you feel you're part of a great continuum—"

"No," he cut her off. "I don't."

"Why not?"

He continued to weave his fingers through her hair. The gesture was less seductive than soothing, as if she were the one with whom he wanted a connection. "It's a long story."

She grinned. "I'm not going anywhere."

Nodding, he collected his thoughts. "My grandfather declared my father dead. There *is* no continuum, not in my family."

"That's terrible, Judd. Why? How did it happen?"

"Well . . ." Taking a deep breath, he told her. "My grandfather was an immigrant from Poland. Aaron Singer, sailing over in steerage at the age of fifteen, ten cents in his pocket and the shirt on his back, et cetera. You know how it goes.''

"I've heard a few variations on the theme."

"When he arrived in New York, he lived in the tenements and supported himself as a street sweeper. Gradually he worked his way up to cleaning buildings instead of streets. He became a janitor. Then he teamed up with a fellow janitor, and they formed a business.''

"Your grandfather sounds very enterprising." *Like his grandson,* she thought.

"So Aaron Singer and Max Moskowitz went into partnership. They did well for themselves. They negotiated contracts to look after some of the sky scrapers going up, hired employees, incorporated. Metro Cleaning Service is still in business. As far as I know, Max's son-in-law runs it now.''

"That's quite a success story," Alana remarked. The myth of the immigrant making good in the New World was a familiar one—her grandfathers on both sides had lived their own versions of it—but it never failed to inspire her.

"My father was supposed to be Max's son-in-law," Judd informed her.

"Oh?"

"Aaron had a son and Max had a daughter, and they worked it all out between them. My father would become a doctor—from immigrant to doctor in one generation—and marry Max's daughter. The old guys had been planning it from the day Max's daughter was born.''

"But . . . ?''

"But while my father was doing his medical internship, he met a nurse."

"Your mother."

"Right."

"And for that your grandfather declared him dead?"

Judd's fingers continued to wander through her hair. "My mother came from a broken home," he said. "She was poor. She'd become a nurse because she had to earn a living. She was a strong, independent woman. My father fell madly in love with her."

"How romantic." Alana sighed. "Not your father losing his family, but the fact that he loved your mother so much."

Judd nodded, evidently agreeing. "When my father couldn't receive his parents' blessing, he and my mother eloped. They were married by a justice of the peace, not a rabbi. That was the final straw. My grandfather disowned him."

"That's so sad."

Another shrug. "It happened," he said simply. "My parents felt there was nothing left for them in New York, so they decided to go as far away as they could."

"Idaho is about as far as you can get."

Judd smiled wryly. "In some ways, I reckon it is."

"Did your father ever make up with his father? After all those years . . ."

"Never. He's a proud man. So is my grandfather. An aunt has kept my father apprised of things—Max's daughter's marriage, my grandfather's retirement, the folks moving to Florida. But there's never been a reconciliation. It's too late.''

Alana almost argued that it was never too late to make peace with one's family, but that would be presumptuous. Judd's father had built his own life with the woman he loved, and he had raised a son. Perhaps Judd had missed out on celebrating the holidays with his family. But he had been blessed with a quick mind and a good soul. Alana had no right to feel sorry for him.

"Damn," he muttered, staring at the stove.

She glanced toward it but saw nothing wrong. "What?"

"I can't believe how tactless I am."

"Tactless?"

He turned back toward her, his gaze brimming with contrition. "Telling you about what my father gave up to be with the woman he loved."

"It's a beautiful story," she reassured him, not certain why he felt he'd been tactless. "I envy your parents."

"Yeah." He turned back to the stove, and she realized he was having trouble looking at her. He must have sensed her bewilderment in her silence, because he muttered, "Your Israeli Air Force pilot."

She understood then. Judd felt bad for pointing out, however inadvertently, that Ben hadn't loved Alana enough to defy his parents for her.

She smiled. "It was for the best that we broke up," she explained. "It hurt at the time, but I don't know how long we would have lasted. His home was in

Haifa. Mine was in Boston. *I* wasn't willing to leave *my* family for him."

"I thought . . . He was the love of your life."

"We did love each other," she admitted. In another context, she might have been amazed to hear herself discuss her love life so candidly with a man—particularly a man she'd kissed with passion not long ago, a man whose virile physique and rugged good looks appealed to her not just as an artist but as a woman. A man whose nearness warmed her and whose distance chilled her. A man with whom she'd lived through hell, with whom she'd lived.

She could tell Judd anything. He could tell her anything. They'd gone too far to worry about tact or taste or anything else. They were sharing a bed, Judd sprawled out and Alana leaning against his legs, as if it were the most natural thing in the world—and right now, it *was* the most natural thing in the world.

"He broke your heart," Judd reminded her.

"I'm a good healer."

He studied her face, then ran his fingertips lightly over her bruised cheek. "In every sense of the word." Slowly, with obvious reluctance, he pushed himself away from her and stood. Alana watched him rummage through the stack of wood they'd brought indoors. When he found the right size log, he opened the firebox and placed it on the blaze. Then he went to the window. "It's so dark out. Like night."

According to Alana's watch, it wasn't yet three o'clock. The violent storm nullified what little sunlight might have seeped through the heavy clouds.

"Don't look," she said, beckoning him back to the cot. "It's too depressing."

"I don't suppose your continuum taught you any prayers about how to end a blizzard?"

"None that I can think of."

He resumed his place on the cot. She stretched out next to him, lying on her back and staring at the spectral shadows that drifted across the ceiling. Judd lay back as he had before. He gazed down at her and asked, in a quiet, intense voice, "Are you afraid?"

She met his probing stare. She knew what he was asking, what fear he was referring to. What *fears*. There were so many of them.

Outside the wind shrieked; the light grew murkier by the second. For all she knew, the entire cabin might wind up buried in the snow, or crushed by an avalanche. Only a fool *wouldn't* be afraid. Only a liar wouldn't admit it.

"Yes," she said. "Are you?"

"Yes." He lifted an errant lock of hair from her cheek and brushed it back behind her ear. "Just before our plane crashed, I saw you working the controls next to me, and I thought, I'm going to die with this woman."

Her heartbeat drummed in her ears. She tried to remember what she'd thought just before the crash: something about keeping the wings level and the nose up, something about hoping the snow would be deep enough to buffer the collision and the clearing large enough to prevent them from smashing into the trees. Something, just before she blacked out, about keeping Judd Singer alive.

And he'd been thinking about dying with her.

Had she thought talking about her ill-fated affair with Ben was intimate? Or discussing the schisms in Judd's family? Or acknowledging her faith? What Judd had just admitted was the most intimate thing anyone had ever said to her.

"Do you think we're going to die?" she asked, looking up into his face and wishing she could make sense of the silver-blue glow animating his eyes.

"I don't want to die," he said. "God knows I'm not ready." He ran his fingers along the edge of her cheek, lifting the feathery wisps of hair away from her temple. "But with you beside me, I can face anything. Even death."

Her heart pounded faster, louder, rattling her ribs the way the storm winds rattled the windowpanes. His fingers touched her skin like tiny flames, burning, leaving a tingling sensation in their wake. Nothing existed beyond his touch, beyond the cot and the fire in the stove. Outside the cabin the blizzard had annihilated the world. All that mattered, all that lived was here, between her and Judd.

She reached for him as he bowed to her, both of them moving at the same time, knowing the same thing. His mouth touched hers, quietly insistent, familiar yet full of discovery. She slid her hand to the back of his head, savoring the silken texture of his tawny hair, the waves curling over the collar of his shirt. Her other hand traced the edge of his jaw, detecting the stubble of beard that had sprouted since last night.

His lips parted on a sigh, and hers parted as well. He wasn't trying to silence her this time, to kiss away her hysteria or her bad dreams. Something in this kiss transcended panic and fear; something spoke of resolution and acceptance. Whatever was to occur at the end of eight days—at the end of this kiss—was their fate. They would get through it together. They had each other.

Their tongues met and merged in the intoxicating heat of their reunion. Alana's fingers twisted through the hair at the nape of Judd's neck, holding him close, rejoicing in the flush of sensation that billowed through her. She and Judd were still very much alive, and as he deepened the kiss she felt even more alive.

"Judd." She heard herself whisper his name, moan it, gasp it as he tilted his head and took full possession of her mouth. He framed her face in his large, strong hands, caressing the underside of her chin with his thumbs as he caressed her tongue with his. He lunged and retreated, skimmed the edge of her teeth and the inner flesh of her lips. He devoured her with a passion she recognized, because she was as much in its thrall as he was.

His hands moved the instant hers did. He traced her shoulders while she explored his back. He cupped her breasts as she gathered fistfuls of cloth, yanking his shirt-tails free of his slacks. He rose higher on her as she brought her hands forward to the buttons of his shirt, tearing at them, needing to feel him.

He groaned as she spread her hands across the warm expanse of his chest, her fingers plowing through the mat of golden curls that covered the upper portion, her palms pressing into the smooth, hard surface of his abdomen. His torso was a glory of muscle and sinew, skin that heated at her touch, nipples that tightened in reflexive pleasure as her fingernails trailed over them. He shucked his shirt in a swift motion, then lifted her sweater and turtleneck over her head. A flick of his fingers unfastened the clasp of her bra, and then he filled his hands with her breasts.

She shuddered as he massaged the rounded flesh, as he caught her nipples between his thumbs and forefingers and tugged gently. She was hot and cold, shivering with a fever of yearning as he grazed a path down her throat to one breast, covered it with his lips and swirled his tongue over the swollen red tip.

His name emerged from her on a breath of agony and delight as he suckled first one breast and then the other. She adored what he was doing and yet she wanted—needed—so much more. Her hips arched restlessly, and he slid his hands under her, holding her to him, rocking her against himself in an unmistakable rhythm.

She shuddered again, deluged with a fluid, rippling heat that flowed through her, gathering where their bodies pressed together. She groped for his belt buckle; he undid the fly and kicked off his trousers, then worked open her jeans and eased them over her hips and off. He gasped when she ran her hand along his aroused flesh, then skimmed his fingers along the sleek outer surface of her thigh to her hip.

She experienced a keen pain that had nothing to do with desire. The cry that escaped her startled them both.

He jerked his hand away. "What?"

"Nothing," she whispered, knowing it was futile. He was already drawing back, gaping at her hip.

"Oh, my God."

"It looks worse than it is," she told him. She had examined the bruise every night when she'd undressed and every morning before putting on her clothes. Her left hip was where the plane's seat belt had done the most damage; days later, the flesh around the jutting bone still looked raw, livid at the center, purple and swollen around it.

"Alana." He bent over and touched his lips tenderly to the hollow above the bruise. The sensation of his lips against her skin sent a tremor down into her womb, so shockingly erotic she lost track of the pain in her hip.

He eased her onto her back and moved his lips over the nearly faded bruises staining the skin of her abdomen. His hands curved around her thighs, glided down and back up, moving her knees apart as his kisses journeyed lower. He shifted to kneel between her legs, then wedged his hands beneath her and lifted her to his mouth.

She cried out again. Every ounce of strength inside her seared a jagged path to where Judd's lips and tongue were conquering her. She seethed, writhed, ached with a desperation she couldn't fathom.

She heard herself protesting, begging, murmuring inchoate pleas as Judd continued to taste and tease and love her. Then everything inside her erupted in a burst of energy, beating relentlessly, pulsing deep into her soul.

She was still moaning as Judd slid up alongside her, drawing the blankets over his body and hers. He rolled onto his back, bringing her with him, guiding her down around him. He entered her with a fierce, possessive thrust and she felt herself burst again, great spasms of sensation surging through her. Her body gripped him, clenched around him as he arched into her. His hands moved up to her breasts, to her hair, pulling her mouth to his for a savage kiss as he convulsed inside her, losing himself to his own overpowering release.

After an eternity the world grew still around her. She heard herself breathing, felt Judd's chest rising and falling beneath her, felt his mouth soften against hers. They were still alive, she thought. They had weathered their own devastating storm. They had illuminated the darkness with their passion, their heat, the sheer joy of their survival.

With you beside me, I can face anything, Judd had said. They had faced this intense, earth-shattering communion, this explosion of need and fear and love.

They'd faced it and triumphed together. Alana understood what miracles and faith were all about.

HE WOULD HAVE BEEN warmer if he'd thrown on his shirt along with his trousers. However, Alana was wearing his shirt right now. The tails fell modestly to her knees in front and back, but they arched up on the sides, revealing tantalizing glimpses of her thighs. Much as he'd prefer that she wear nothing at all, he didn't want her to catch cold—and he certainly didn't want her to get dressed.

Nor did he want to put on another shirt, not while he was still reliving the feel of her hands on him. Her touch had been light at first, almost shy. But as her hunger had built she'd become less inhibited, digging her fingertips into the small of his back, into the hard muscles of his buttocks, stroking through the hair on his chest and down, capturing and captivating him with a single electrifying caress.

He wanted her, again. More than before. More than he could remember ever wanting anything.

But the cabin had grown dark, and there was a fire to revive in the stove, a bit of rabbit stew to reheat, a candle to light.

She roamed through the kitchen area, illuminating the space with the everlasting kerosene lamp. Judd fiddled with the logs in the firebox, shifting a charred one and propping a fresh one above it. When he closed the firebox and straightened up, he saw her bowed over the flickering candle on the counter, reciting her nightly Hanukkah prayer.

"Blessed art Thou, oh Lord, our God," she began. The candlelight bathed her face, magnifying the hypnotic darkness of her eyes, the lushness of her lips. "Judd thinks there's no such thing as magic, but I'm not so sure. Thank You, God, for Your magic."

Glancing up, she saw him watching her and smiled bashfully. Then she busied herself gathering plates and forks.

She was so beautiful, he thought. So full of trust.

He stirred the stew absently, his mind on other things. On Alana. On why he, ordinarily not a very trusting soul, wanted to be worthy of her trust. On why he wanted so much.

He never felt like this with other women. He liked his relationships calm and easy. Any demands made were superficial: a glitzy outing for New Year's Eve; a suitably charming companion at business functions. Judd wanted someone who wouldn't throw a fit if he had to cancel a date at the last minute; Susan wanted someone who treated her with respect and satisfied her in bed. They enjoyed each other's company. And that was that.

His gaze traveled back to Alana and stayed with her, following her as she glided between the kitchen area and the table. If only she would make demands on him, he would gladly fulfill them, exceed them. He was willing to do anything for her, to make any sacrifice she demanded of him.

But she would never demand a thing.

They didn't talk much as they ate. She sat across the table from him, looking utterly irresistible in the oversize shirt, the sleeves cuffed several times to reach her wrists and the collar yawning open whenever she leaned forward. She picked at her stew, apparently not hungry.

It worried him that she wasn't eating more. She had no excess fat on her, and the stew might be the last meat they'd have for a while. He didn't expect to be able to bring down another rabbit as easily as he'd brought down this one. Especially after the storm. If they were as severely snowed in as he suspected, they would be living on pretzels and soup until they dug themselves out.

Which might take days.

"Are you all right?" he asked.

She looked up. The shimmering darkness of her eyes took his breath away. "Fishing for compliments?" she shot back with a mischievous grin.

Her teasing had a predictable effect on his body. He shifted in his chair to relieve the pressure. "Eat," he said, indicating her barely touched food.

"Don't be a mother," she warned, still grinning.

"Can I get you something else? Do you want some oatmeal?"

"Judd, please. I'm fine." She extended her leg under the table and propped her bare foot on his knee. He nearly dropped his fork.

"Then why aren't you eating?" he asked in an admirably level voice.

"I'm too content," she said.

He hadn't known it was possible to be *too* content. Particularly when death lurked in every gale, in every crystal of ice that descended from the sky. Yet Alana looked blessedly at peace. He realized with a sudden stab of insight that she hadn't placed her foot in his lap to turn him on. She'd done it because she'd wanted to make contact with him, to build a connection between them.

His body relaxed and he attacked his food, feeling less aroused, more serene. She could eat or not eat. He could make love with her or not. What mattered was that she was touching him, bridging the space between them, connecting with him even when the task of eating separated them.

They were united. They were together. That was the most important thing.

THEY FELL ASLEEP in what Judd now considered their official position, both on their sides, Alana with her back to him, one of his arms wrapped comfortably around her and the other tucked under her pillow. Tonight, no sweatshirt came between her smooth, silky back and his chest; skin touched skin as he pressed himself into the soft, round flesh of her bottom. Her hair flowed around her shoulders, across his chin. Her breast filled his hand.

They had confronted the blizzard one last time before retiring to bed. It had been an arduous hike to the outhouse. The lamp actually threatened to go out as the wind tore across the opening at the top of the glass chimney. But the wick, though guttering, stayed lit as he and Alana staggered through the treacherous snow. By the time they'd returned to the cabin, they were exhausted, panting as if they'd run a marathon.

Tomorrow would be better, he resolved, hugging her to himself and relishing the soothing lull of her breathing, the warmth of her body curled within the arch of his. Tomorrow the storm would be over, and they would clear their way out of the cabin, and he would find the trail down from the mountains. Or a helicopter would find them. Enough was enough; if God really could perform magic, let Him put on a magic show for His two stranded servants.

Judd needed to be in New York. He could picture the frenzy his absence must be causing. His friends and colleagues probably assumed he was dead. He had to get back and reclaim his life. He had to resume his normal existence. That was what he wanted, wasn't it?

He'd had it with miracles and the lack of them. He'd had it with the screaming wind and the daggers of ice thrashing the windows. He'd had it with wood fires and the lack of plumbing, electricity, books and newspapers, fresh bagels and...what had he and Alana fantasized about? Brownies a la mode?

He wanted out of here. He wanted his life back.

In her sleep, Alana sighed, and all his wants coalesced into one single, burning need. Her breast seemed to swell against his hand as she inhaled. He felt the stiff point of her nipple, as smooth and taut as a bead, and chafed it with his thumb.

She moaned, twisting against him and letting her head fall back against his shoulder. He pressed his lips to the skin below her ear and she moaned again.

He recalled the first time he had joined her in bed. She had been rigid with fear until he'd gathered her to himself, bending his knees behind hers and enveloping her with his arms. Gradually she'd unwound, softening against him, molding herself to him and making him half mad with desire.

Every night that he'd lain with her this way the madness had seized him. He could have her now; she was stretching, trailing her toes along his shin, turning her head so he could kiss her throat and shoulder. Her eyes blinked open and she tried to rotate to face him.

"No," he whispered, sliding his hand from her breast to her waist and holding her back against him. He browsed along the delicate ridge of her shoulder to the nape of her neck, shoving her hair out of his way. She surged, once more trying to turn around, but he held her firm. With another sigh she subsided, resting in the circle of his arms.

He skimmed his hands lower, from her waist across her belly, skirting her hips to avoid the bruises. He caressed her thighs, then slid one hand between her legs, through the soft, downy curls. She twitched as his fingers found her, found the damp darkness of her, took possession, released her and then took her again. A choked sob tore from her throat as her hips danced to his tempo.

"Judd..." She clamped her hands onto his forearms, flexing and pinching as he deepened his caress. "Judd...please..."

"Like this," he murmured, kissing her earlobe, her shoulders, the base of her neck. Easing her onto her stomach, he pulled her up against him, penetrating, filling her. Her gasp of ecstasy nearly robbed him of what little control he had.

She was so tight, so hot. He kept one arm firm around her waist; his other hand remained where it was, moving on her as he moved within her. She shuddered beneath him, the pillows muffling her cries as he urged her onward, as his response fed off hers. He felt her trembling, hovering, and then she went limp, her body undulating around him, drawing him deeper and deeper into his own unbearable pleasure.

No longer able to contain himself, he let go in a final, wrenching thrust. His groan mixed with Alana's as he crested, pulsing fire, blazing into her soul. Long after he was spent he felt her throbbing around him, tensing and relaxing in a secret, womanly rhythm.

He bowed to kiss her shoulders once more, the lissome curves and hollows of her back. She grew motionless beneath him, her breath gradually returning to normal, her fingers unfurling against the sheets. He wanted to say something, laugh with her, reassure her. Reassure himself.

Slowly, he lifted himself off her and turned her to face him. Her eyes were wide, her cheeks streaked with tears. As she reached up he lowered himself into her arms and held her tight.

There were demands, now, demands too deep for words. Demands he felt but didn't understand. Demands coming from her, coming from inside himself, coming from the wild storm that held them prisoner in the cabin's shadows. The demands of life and death, despair and hope.

As he lay within her arms, bound to her in too many ways to name, he realized how truly lost he was.

Chapter Ten

Alana awakened to sunshine, to peace.

Pushing away from the pillow, she discovered the cabin awash in a milky light as the morning sun battled through the snowdrifts outside the cabin's windows. Where yesterday she had heard the constant roar of the storm, today she heard nothing but silence.

Judd stirred beside her. Turning, she watched him open his eyes. He regarded her warily, then gave her a hesitant smile and pulled her back down to the pillow, into his arms. She cuddled up within his sleepy embrace and thought about what awaited them once they arose.

The sunlight indicated a fair sky, perfect for helicopters. No doubt the plane wreckage was buried under a foot of fresh snow, but she and Judd could sweep off the wing and exhume the red plaid blanket—if it hadn't blown away. They could work together, preparing for their rescue.

Then, once they lured a helicopter to the clearing, they would be able to return to the real world. She would be able to go home to Boston, to her cozy loft in Cambridge. And Judd would go home to New York. To his girlfriend.

Of course. That was how it was supposed to be. They were enduring this entire grievous episode in the hope that eventually they would be able to go home, back to their normal, separate lives.

Yesterday, confronted with their own mortality, they had reached for life in the most elemental way. But that didn't mean Alana had forgotten about Judd's life back in New York. Not even when they had been locked together in the most profound, primal intimacy had she let the truth slip her mind.

Well, maybe she had, just a little.

More than a little.

All right. Maybe she'd been thinking of love when Judd had worked his magic on her. Maybe, after eating with him, sleeping with him, walking and working with him and, finally, making love with him, she had allowed notions of forever to sneak into her brain.

But sooner or later they were going to leave the mountain, and she'd have to rid herself of those notions.

"It looks like a nice morning," she said, her lips brushing idly against the springy hair on Judd's chest.

He sighed and twined his fingers through her thick dark tresses. "It's going to be a disaster out there."

"A sunny disaster, at least."

"Cold and messy."

"We'll bundle up."

He pulled his hand from her hair and drew back. Again she detected wariness in his expression, something chilly and distant. Abruptly he turned, threw back the covers and reached for his slacks.

He was coming to terms with the facts, acknowledging that last night was gone and a new day had broken. And he was retreating. Whenever she got close he ran away, and last night they'd been so close. Much too close.

She reached for his shirt, which lay in a wrinkled heap on the floor on her side of the cot. Running her hands over the soft, thick chamois, she remembered the way it had felt on her, brushing her breasts as gently as a lover's lips. She hastily handed it to him.

His gaze intersected with hers as he took it. "Alana," he murmured, his tone hinting at need and regret and a dozen other, less easily identified emotions.

She gathered her own clothes and concentrated on getting dressed as quickly as possible. "We managed not to use up all the wood," she remarked brightly as she gestured toward the three unused logs by the stove. "Why don't you get the fire started, and I'll make some coffee."

After zipping her slacks, she headed toward the kitchen. Judd snagged her arm as she passed him. Spinning her around, he planted his hands on her shoulders and peered down into her face.

"Are you all right?"

"Why shouldn't I be all right?"

He flexed his lips, searching for the right words. "I feel like I should say something."

"How about, thanks for the good time?"

He closed his eyes for a moment, absorbing the brittle cheer in her tone. "Yesterday was special, Alana. You have to know that. Everything that happened between us was special."

She'd thought it had been magic. Well, she sighed, no point arguing over semantics. Judd didn't believe in magic. And whatever either of them wanted to call it, it was over. Past tense. Yesterday.

He loosened his grip and moved his fingers gently over her shoulders. "I wouldn't take a moment of it back. It's something I'll never forget."

A kiss-off if ever she heard one. "Fine," she said, presenting him with a smile as phony as it was bright. "I'll make some coffee now."

He let her go, but she felt his gaze following her as she moved through the kitchen area, ladling water out of the basin, measuring coffee grounds from the can. Maybe *she* was the one running away now. But he'd run first. The instant her eyes had met his in bed, she'd felt his withdrawal. He was running as fast as he could.

She would survive this, too. If she could survive a plane crash she could survive anything.

He laced his boots and strode to the door. She glanced over her shoulder in time to see him open it. Snow had piled waist-high on the other side. The mound spilled into the cabin, and he grabbed the broom and shoved it back out. "We don't have a shovel, do we?" he asked.

"I haven't found one."

Slinging his arms through his jacket, he grabbed the broom and climbed over what was left of the drift, tugging the door shut behind him.

Gone, she thought, feeling another wave of misery wash over her. She sternly shook it off. Really, what had she expected? A marriage proposal?

Of course not. But a kiss might have been nice. A kiss, a touch, a physical acknowledgment of the wonder he and Alana had shared last night. Maybe passion like that was an everyday occurrence to him, but to her...

To her it had been life itself. Proof that in spite of everything she and Judd were still alive. It had been a merging of their lives, a communion of their souls.

She mustn't torture herself with poetic interpretations. What happened had happened. It had been special, but now it was over. She prayed for a rescue helicopter to arrive soon, so she wouldn't have to spend a minute longer than necessary with Judd.

He returned to the cabin when the oatmeal was starting to thicken. "It's awful out there," he said, stomping the snow off his boots and removing his jacket.

"Did you check the clearing?"

He nodded. "The plane is buried under a ton of snow."

She spooned the cereal into two bowls and set them on the table. "A ton isn't much," she joked, determined not to let her heartache show. "We can clean it off in an hour."

"*We?*"

"Sure. If we work together—"

"I'll do it. You'll stay inside."

She ate a spoonful of oatmeal, giving her temper time to cool off. "*I* will clean off the plane," she said, enunciating each word with care. "You can either help me or not."

"No." His pale, cool eyes bore down on her from across the table.

"Judd—"

"I saw you," he cut her off. "I saw the bruises. You haven't given yourself a chance to heal, Alana. You've got to take it easy."

He'd seen the bruises when he was making love to her. And this was the outcome—not love but protectiveness, patronizing, paternalistic smothering, a reproach about how she wasn't taking it easy enough.

"Thank you, Dr. Singer," she snapped. "I'll decide when and how I want to heal."

His tone was as placating as hers was sharp. "Alana, be reasonable. The snow is very deep, and you haven't got any boots. It's hard to walk through the stuff. I was skidding and sinking in, and I'm a lot taller than you. You're going to fall and hurt yourself—"

"I'm going to do whatever the hell I feel like doing," she retorted, shoving her bowl away and rising to her feet. How dare he try to baby her? How dare he play the chivalrous gentleman, protecting her from the big, bad world? Alana had gotten herself through seven nations of Europe without help. She'd earned her way, extricated herself from sticky predicaments, journeyed to Israel, fallen in love, returned to Boston and healed just fine, without any help from anyone.

She'd landed a good-paying job and found a charming residence in Cambridge. She painted paintings and flew airplanes.

And when she wanted to go out in the snow, that was exactly what she did.

Wedging her feet into her loafers, she snatched her jacket from the rocker and yanked it on. Judd sprang out of his chair and raced over to her. "Alana. It's sunny out there, but it's bitter cold and dangerous."

"Leave me alone," she muttered, fussing with the buttons on her jacket. Judd was bitter cold and dangerous, too. She'd probably be safer outdoors than with him. "Why don't you go find the trail?"

"I will, after I clear off the plane. And you will stay here and wait."

"Like hell."

"Use your head, Alana! Don't go out."

She had to use her heart as well as her head. Her heart told her that if she wasn't in control of her life, staying alive would no longer matter. It told her that reality was this morning, not last night, that reality was Judd Singer the detached businessman, not Judd Singer the passionate lover.

She had always been independent, strong, fearless. No one was going to take that away from her—certainly not Judd. He had already taken too much.

Wrapping her scarf around her neck, she headed for the door. Judd clamped his hand on her shoulder; she shrugged it off. "You do what you have to do," she said, her voice gritty with resolution. "I'll do what I have to do."

At that moment, what she had to do was forge into the sun-glazed snow, alone and unafraid, and prove to herself that Judd hadn't stolen her will along with everything else.

DAMN IT! Why couldn't she let him handle things? Why couldn't she take it easy?

Why was she so hell-bent on hurting herself even more?

Sighing, he lifted his mug from the table and added some hot coffee to the tepid dregs. He stood at the window and sipped, working through his thoughts.

His quick jaunt outside earlier had informed him he wouldn't find a trail back to civilization any time soon, not with the dense, heavy layer of snow that had fallen over the mountain. He could head out in the direction of the marked trees, but he didn't expect to find much, not with everything obliterated by snowdrifts.

Surveying the cabin, he settled his vision on the gun rack. They needed food. Meat. He wondered if protein deprivation caused insanity.

He pulled down a rifle and crossed to the kitchen to collect the shells and hunting knife. Alana would come to her senses soon. The cold would get to her and she'd return to the cabin, leaving the job of exhuming the plane to him. If luck was with him, he would have shot something edible by the time she returned to the cabin. He would fix her a substantial meal and make her rest.

He would take care of her, whether she liked it or not.

SHE DIDN'T CARE. She just didn't care. She had to get out of here, away from this horrible mountain. If it meant digging up every cubic inch of snow in the clearing, she would do it.

The morning air was outrageously cold, and walking was difficult. Her feet alternately slid along the surface crust of ice or sank deep into the snow, tossing her about, forcing her to contort her body to stay erect.

But she wouldn't stop, wouldn't slow down. She was the pilot; the plane was her responsibility. Judd could do whatever the hell he wanted, but the plane was hers.

Armed with a bucket from the cabin, she scrambled across the white hills that had formed over pieces of the plane. Scooping away the snow, she experienced a small thrill whenever she struck metal, rubber or glass.

The largest hill covered the bulk of the fuselage. That was where she concentrated her efforts. Her shoes and slacks stayed relatively dry; the snow was too cold to melt and saturate them. Her hands were protected by her gloves, her head by her scarf.

She dug harder, deeper, smashing her fists the entire length of the wing to loosen the ice and then swiping huge chunks of frozen snow from the wing flaps. Thinking of Judd made her pound harder, work faster. He was as cold as the snow, and she derived a cathartic satisfaction from banging and shoving and wiping away the treacherous stuff.

Last night had offered her a powerful reminder of what it meant to be alive. Today's exercise made her feel just as alive. In its own way, anger was every bit as potent as love.

THE TWO SQUIRRELS Judd shot added up to less meat than the one rabbit he'd nailed two days ago. It had taken him several hours to scare up the scrawny critters, but he'd gotten them.

He'd had to hike deep into the forest in search of prey, and his hike back out, with the rifle slung over his shoulder and the squirrel flesh packed in snow, took over a half hour. The air was so cold his nostrils felt stiff from breathing it; ice crystals accumulated in his eyebrows and along the bristle of his beard. His fingertips hurt, his ears smarted. But soon he'd be cooking up a mess of meat, feeding himself and Alana, stoking up on fuel for his foray back out in search of the trail.

He entered the cabin to find it empty. No Alana. All he saw was the cot where they had tested the limits of passion, where they'd renewed themselves in each other's arms and discovered themselves in each other's souls. The sight of it revived Judd's memories of the previous night. Groaning, he turned away.

Where was she?

Exiting the cabin, he followed Alana's tracks to the clearing. The plane stood nearly completely visible, its intact wing and entire right side exposed to the sun.

No sign of Alana.

He couldn't discern a single trail of footprints in the clearing; she'd obviously been marching every which way, tossing and scattering the snow. He circled the plane just to be sure she hadn't stalked off into the woods on the other side of the field. She hadn't.

He returned to the passenger side of the plane, noting absently that she'd done an excellent job cleaning the snow off the fuselage. Worry gnawed at him. What if she'd slipped and banged her head and somehow had gotten buried in a snowbank? What if a huge chunk of ice had slid from the roof of the plane and hit her in the head?

He approached the plane cautiously, searching the mounds of snow at his feet. Within a yard of the passenger door, he spotted her through the window. She was in the passenger seat, curled up on her side, her knees drawn to her chest and her head resting against one arm. When he pulled open the door she barely turned her head. Her eyes fluttered but didn't focus on him. Her lips were blue.

"Alana?"

She lowered her head to her arm and sighed.

He shoved back the door, reached in and dragged her to the edge of the seat, then into his arms. Her teeth began to chatter and she closed her eyes. "Tired," she mumbled, nuzzling her head into his jacket.

A million curses scorched his tongue. The idiot! The stupid, stubborn, brainless idiot! Didn't she know how dangerous hypothermia was? She could die out here!

Tightening his arms around her, he staggered across the clearing. Through her jacket he felt her shivering, snuggling her icy body closer to him. He nearly lost his footing as he entered the forest, but he caught himself on a tree, took a deep breath and then hurried through the woods to the cabin.

Inside, he gave the door a violent kick to shut it, then carried her to the cot and dropped her onto it. She immediately curled back into fetal position, but he yanked her legs straight and stripped off her soggy shoes and socks, her clammy slacks, her jacket and sweater.

"I'm tired," she moaned as he collected his sweat-shirt, sweatpants and wool socks from his duffel bag. "So tired..."

He dressed her as quickly as he could in the dry garments, then wrapped the blankets around her until she looked like an oversize papoose. Her lips were still blue, her eyes swimming.

"What the hell were you thinking of?" he railed, grabbing the percolator and slamming it onto the stove to reheat the leftover coffee. "Why did you stay out-side?"

"I didn't," she said, her tone muffled, as if her tongue were coated in cotton. "I went in."

"Into the airplane. You should have come here. I thought you were an intelligent woman, Alana, but this has to be one of the stupidest things..." He poured a mug half-full of warm coffee, brought it to the cot, propped her up against himself in a sitting position and lifted the mug to her lips. "Take a sip."

She moved her lips, then shook her head. "Too tired."

"Drink!"

She sipped, then coughed, an ominous, rattling cough deep in her lungs. "Let me sleep," she pleaded, closing her eyes and lowering her head.

"Do you know what hypothermia is?"

"Go away."

"Listen to me, damn it. You could die."

"So what's new?"

He bit his lip to stifle his rage. Through the layers of clothing and blankets he could feel her trembling against him, her slim, fragile body shuddering in a way that alarmed him. He was scolding her out of panic, out of abject fear.

He might lose her. She could die. Dear God, she could have survived the crash only to die from the cold.

He tried to force more coffee into her mouth, but she resisted, coughing and turning her face away. "I'm going to make you some soup," he said, rising from the cot. Alana rolled up on her side and buried her head in the pillow.

His hands shook. When he'd thought she was dead right after the crash, he'd been upset, but not like this. She'd been a virtual stranger to him them. She'd been a pilot and a representative from Neeley, Henderson. Now...

Now she was Alana Halpern. The most exasperating woman he'd ever met. The craziest. The boldest. The sexiest.

Oh, God, if she died...

He stirred the soup like a fiend, clanking the spoon against the sides of the pot. Grabbing a bowl from the dry sink, he served up a portion, returned to the cot and propped her up against himself once more. "Eat this," he said.

Her eyes still shut, she sank limply against him and groaned.

"Eat it, Alana."

"No."

He took some of the broth into the spoon and pressed it against her lips. "Eat it."

She opened her mouth to speak, and he shoveled the spoon in. She made a gagging noise, then swallowed and coughed again. "Stop!" she pleaded in a hoarse, rusty tone.

He was pushing too hard. Maybe if she warmed up her appetite would improve. *If* she warmed up...

She *had* to warm up. He refused to acknowledge any other outcome.

Setting the soup bowl on the counter, he returned to the cot and gathered Alana to himself. The blankets and his sweatsuit added bulk to her slender form; she shivered wildly in his arms.

"You're supposed to combat hypothermia with hot fluids," he explained, tightening his hold on her as if he could warm her up by sheer will.

Her breath was shallow. Her lips were still blue, her teeth still chattering.

He rubbed her shoulders through the layers of material insulating her body. "Alana," he whispered, wondering whether she heard him. "Damn it, Alana— why do you have to be so stubborn?"

A long minute elapsed between her breaths. He gave her a frantic shake and she inhaled. She felt so cold, so frightfully cold.

"Why did you risk your life?" he asked, knowing she wouldn't answer.

He tried to answer for her: she'd risked her life to be contrary. He'd asked her to stay indoors, so she'd gone out. She'd done it to spite him.

She'd done it because she no longer trusted him.

She'd done it because she hated him, because she'd rather die than spend another minute alone on this desolate mountain with him.

She'd done it because of what had happened last night.

Why? he thought. *Why?* Where the hell was God when they needed Him? Giving bad directions to the rescue crews? Churning up another blizzard? Laughing derisively at His two struggling servants, His victims?

What had they done to deserve this?

He massaged her neck. He sandwiched her legs between his, pressed her body to his, prayed for his warmth to reach her. He rocked her in his arms and touched his lips to her brow. He wished he had one of those silly wands that were such hot sellers in the Magic Shops, and he could wave it over her bowed head and make everything right.

But there was no magic, no guarantee. There was nothing but fear. Nothing but the endless world of snow, and this cabin, and this cot that had already witnessed too many intimacies.

There was nothing but his arms around her, holding her, trying to keep her alive and knowing everything he could do might not be enough.

Chapter Eleven

For the rest of the afternoon she drifted in and out of consciousness.

When she was asleep, Judd huddled behind her, adding his body heat to whatever warmth she got from the blankets. Frequently she shivered; occasionally she moaned, besieged by nightmares Judd could only begin to imagine.

When she opened her eyes, he would leave the cot for the kitchen. He would bring her small portions of warm soup and slivers of squirrel meat. Alana would struggle to consume a few spoonfuls of the soup, then pull the blankets around her like a cocoon and let the nightmares claim her once more. Judd would lie beside her, gathering her trembling body to himself and wishing he could fight off her demons for her.

Her temperature rose from chilly to feverish. She sweated, mumbled, flinched in a delirium of anguish. Sometimes he was able to make out a few words: *No.... Come back.... Judd.*

Then she would open her unseeing eyes again, and he would wash her face with a damp paper towel, try to force some soup into her, and tell himself over and over that she was going to be all right. Her complexion was sallow, her lips parched, her eyes sunken in shadow.

The sun set, leaving behind long shadows and a starlit sky. He rose and lit the kerosene lamp. He should have been astonished that after so many days and so little fuel the wick still ignited, but he was too angry to be astonished. If there had to be a miracle, why couldn't it be Alana's? Why should the lamp still have life in it while she continued to hover near death?

He added some wood to the firebox and stood a candle in the ashtray. He couldn't care less if they had their silly Hanukkah ritual tonight, but he'd beg for miracles if that was what it took.

"Don't," she whispered.

He spun around and found her lying on her side, watching him.

"Don't what?" he asked, going to her and kneeling beside her.

"The candle." Speaking the words seemed to exhaust her. With a long, weary breath, she sank into the pillows and looked away.

He wanted to grab her by the shoulders, shake her and shout that she mustn't give up. She was a fighter, and now, more than ever, she needed her fighting spirit. "It's the fifth night of Hanukkah," he reminded her.

She closed her eyes and drifted into unconsciousness once more.

A hard, bitter lump filled his throat. It wasn't supposed to be like this. Alana was the optimist, the one who believed in God and magic and the magnificence of the holiday. She was the one who filled the cabin with hope, the one who counteracted his cynicism. He kept the fire alive in the stove, and she kept the fire alive everywhere else, with her artwork, her cooking skill, her beauty and her faith.

If she gave up, how on earth was Judd supposed to keep going?

"Let me light it," he implored, stroking his fingers tenderly over her cheeks, into her damp, tangled hair.

She lay motionless, her breath labored, her fingers clutching the blanket around her.

He didn't light it. Without her, what was the point?

The next time she awakened, he managed to get her to consume a few spoonfuls of soup. Later, he warmed some water and bathed her face and hands. As he ran the wet towels over her cheeks and throat she simply stared at him, her eyes dull, her respiration harsh and unnervingly irregular. Her fingers lay limp against his palms as he washed and dried them.

"We're going to be rescued," he said, not because he believed it but because he had to restore her hope.

Her only response was to shut her eyes and sigh.

"We're going to be rescued, and you're going to be fine." *I won't let anything happen to you,* he almost said, but that would have been an even bigger lie. Never in his life had he felt as helpless as he did now. No matter how much soup and meat he forced into her, he couldn't cure her. Magic was beyond him.

He poured out the wash water and stretched on the cot beside her. While she slept and moaned and struggled through the night, he held her and wondered how—if—they would make it through another day.

He felt utterly lost, embattled by his own demons. Through the blankets he felt Alana's frail, quivering body and his heart threatened to tear in two. He had never needed faith until now—and faith had abandoned him. He couldn't bear this much pain.

Closing his eyes, closing his arms around Alana, he prayed to a god he couldn't believe in that the pain would go away. Even if it meant he had to stop feeling, stop caring, stop hoping. He just wanted the pain to go away.

THE COLD roused him.

Pushing away from the mattress, he gazed around the cabin. The first pale hint of dawn seeped through the windows from the east. Dust motes swirled through the shafts of sunlight.

The stove was out, the cabin silent. Alana's breathing had lost its scratchy sound.

He sat higher and peered down at her. The blankets had loosened slightly at her throat, and her hair spilled in lush black waves around her face. Her skin had lost its pallor. Her lips, parted in an alluring way, were a healthy pink.

He touched the inside of his wrist to her brow. Her fever had broken.

He rolled his head from side to side to loosen the stiff muscles in his neck. Rising from the cot, he noticed the unlit candle standing in the ashtray, a silent reproach.

He scrubbed his fingers through his hair and searched the room for his boots. He had to get a fire going, pump some caffeine into his system and then, once Alana was awake, he would set back out on that red-paint trail and find a way to save them both from this place before it destroyed them.

Grabbing his jacket, he swung out the door. The heavy, treaded sole of his boots crunched into the packed snow as he walked to the overhang.

One split log.

Every morning there had been an adequate supply of firewood waiting for him. Alana considered it a miracle; he had simply accepted it with gratitude.

This morning there was only one log, and a short, stubby branch beside it.

Finding the woodpile each morning had spoiled him; now he was on his own.

He surveyed the surrounding forest. Snow covered whatever wood might be lying on the ground, and the few pine trees near the cabin wore all their greenery high up on their trunks. Stifling a curse, Judd snapped off the dried lower branches and carried them into the cabin. Alana was still fast asleep.

Inside the firebox was a partially burned log to which he added the pine twigs and the fresh log. After lighting the fire, he grabbed a knife and went back out.

The barren space under the overhang taunted him as he strode past it, just as the unlit candle in the ashtray had taunted him when he'd hurried through the kitchen.

He hiked to the clearing to check on the debris as he foraged for wood. The plaid blanket lashed to the wing had faded. He wondered if its color was vivid enough to attract attention from above. As if its pre-faded brightness had done them any good before.

He leaned against the frosted wing and stared at the snow. If he ever got out of here, he'd move to Hawaii. He never wanted to see snow again, as long as he lived.

For all he knew, he might not have long to live.

The breeze nipped at him. Digging his hands into his pockets, he discovered the knife in one, and in the other the small chunk of wood he'd found under the overhang. He studied the wood, gauging its shape, then he began to whittle.

He had always put his trust in reality, but that morning reality was too bleak to stomach. The firewood was gone.

It had to mean something.

He wished he knew how to pray. What were those words Alana began her prayers with? *Blessed art Thou, King of the Universe* . . .

Frankly, Judd was not enamored of this universe. It was cold and cruel, and the only warmth in it came from a woman who had the ability to scramble his brain waves, to make him think and act in ways that bore no relationship to who he used to be.

He was an outsider, a kid who had won the respect of his peers with his fists and his wits because they wouldn't respect him for what he was. He had been as solitary throughout his life as he was at that moment, standing alone in a field of snow, aching to attract attention from above.

Just what kind of attention did he want to attract? What did he expect to rescue him? A helicopter or God? Helicopters were reality, science, logic—and helicopters had failed. How could he keep believing in them?

Shavings of wood curled against the blade of his knife and dropped at his feet. As he whittled the stick he whittled his thoughts, stripping off the dingy outer bark and trying to mold them into a new shape.

Somewhere in the distance, he heard the caw of a crow. The wind whistled through the trees.

"I don't know how to pray," he said aloud.

If he and Alana were going to die, why couldn't they have died in the plane crash? What could God have hoped to accomplish by allowing them to live, to grow close, to make love—to have their friendship tainted by fear, anger, the constant threat of death? Where was the sense of it?

Why did Alana have to suffer? What kind of a God would put a woman like her through such torture?

"If I have to die, fine," he said, hacking at the chunk of wood in his hands. "Just let her live. Let her be all right." A slab of wood fell from the knife and hit the snow with a faint thud. "My life for hers, God. It's a fair deal."

He carved the wood, waiting for something: enlightenment, comprehension, an epiphany. Attention from above.

Minutes passed. The crow cawed again, a harsh, lonesome cry through the forest. The piece of wood had shrunk until it fit in the curve of Judd's palm. For the first time since he'd started chiseling it he examined what he was creating. He had whittled the branch into a square tapering to a point on one end and a knob at the other.

A dreidel.

Great, he snorted under his breath. He was waiting for a sign from above, some profound, eternal insight regarding God and the meaning of life. And what did he get? A little Hanukkah toy.

As he recalled, a dreidel was supposed to have four Hebrew letters on it, one adorning each of the four faces. He had no idea what the letters were—in fact, he knew nothing about the Hebrew alphabet. He must have seen enough pictures of dreidels in his life, though, because he visualized the letters. He etched their shapes into the wood, smoothed it a bit and spun it in his hand.

Judd had a dreidel. But he still didn't have firewood, a way off the mountain or an understanding of why he and Alana had wound up here, where they were going, how this would end.

Skip the philosophy, he ordered himself. Accumulating firewood was the most important thing.

He trudged across the field toward the cabin. Within a few yards of it he stumbled to a halt. There, beneath the overhang, was a neat pyramid of split logs.

He cursed, then laughed, then cursed again. The pile was too visible, too obvious for him to have overlooked earlier. He couldn't have missed it. Yet for the wood to appear all by itself didn't make sense.

But then, nothing made sense anymore.

In the cabin, as he laid one of the logs in the stove, he heard a sigh behind him and the rustling of bed linens. He turned and saw Alana blink awake, then push back the blankets. Her eyes looked clear and bright, the glaze of illness gone from them.

"Good morning," he said.

"Good morning."

Her smile flooded him with heat. She was alive, alert, radiant. He didn't believe in miracles or magic...but *something* had happened. Alana's strength was restored, and they had wood. It didn't matter what Judd believed. *Something* had happened.

He unzipped his jacket and sat on the cot. "How do you feel?"

"Better," she said. "Good."

"Here." He pulled the dreidel out of his pocket and presented it to her. Then, suddenly embarrassed, he went over to the table, where he busied himself removing his jacket and snow-covered boots.

The lengthy silence prompted him to glance her way. She was sitting up, her disheveled hair framing her face in a lush tumble of black, the too-large sweatshirt drooping along one shoulder and the blankets bunching around her waist. She cradled the carved wood in her hands, turning it, studying it, smiling a secret smile.

At last she lifted her face. He couldn't help responding to the unadorned joy in her eyes.

"Do you know what this is?" she asked as he returned to the cot and sat beside her.

"A dreidel."

"An Israeli dreidel."

"What do you mean? It's a New Hampshire dreidel."

She smiled and shook her head. "Look what it says. Everywhere except in Israel, a dreidel would have a *shin* here." She pointed to one of the letters. "The letters are supposed to be *nun, gimel, hey,* and *shin.* But you didn't put a *shin* here. You put a *pe.*"

He frowned. He wouldn't know a *shin* from a *pe,* or any of the other letters she was identifying.

"The letters stand for *Nes gadol haya sham.* It means, 'A great miracle happened *there,*' meaning the miracle happened in Jerusalem."

"Okay." This was news to him. He'd always thought the letters stood for how many candies or pennies a person gambling with a dreidel could take out of the kitty.

"But in Israel," she explained in her velvety voice, "they use a *pe* because the letters stand for *Nes gadol haya po.* That means, 'A great miracle happened *here.*'"

He peered into her face. Her eyes were alive with light, with bright sparks of pleasure.

He wasn't convinced that miracles happened here, there or anywhere else. He felt overwhelmed by the questions hammering at him. But he had a lifetime to seek the answers—if he didn't die on this mountain.

And if he did, the answers wouldn't matter.

Alana's eyes grew brighter, drawing him in. Her mouth softened in a smile. At that one moment, a lifetime in itself, he knew the only answer that existed.

ALANA NEEDED HIS KISS the way she'd needed him throughout her wretched night. He had been a life force, staving off her chills, protecting her against the raging dreams. He had forfeited his own comfort, provided her with blankets and sleepwear and what little body warmth he could offer. He had given himself to her.

What happened next was irrelevant. All that counted was now, this miracle happening here.

In the past, his kisses had been fraught with desperation. This kiss was slow, tranquil, beguiling. It was a whisper of lips against lips, a feathery stroke of his fingertips against her cheek, the reflection of his heat and strength inside her. Her lips brushed his; his coaxed hers. When his hand moved deep into her hair she sighed and relaxed, opening her mouth to him.

His tongue made a playful foray past her teeth. His moan spoke only of satisfaction, not terror or distress.

The room was filled with daylight, with the cozy warmth of the fire in the stove. The last traces of her turbulent night evaporated like mist in the morning sun. Reaching for Judd, she ran her fingers over his beard—now three days old, it had lost its stubbly roughness. He lowered her back to the pillow, his lips never leaving hers.

She felt him part the blankets around her, felt his hands moving in slow, sweeping paths down her body. He kicked his legs up onto the cot, and she tugged his shirt free of his trousers and slipped her hands inside. She wanted to feel the chest that had radiated its healing heat around her all night. *A miracle happened here,* she thought, molding her hands to the thick arch of his rib cage, her tongue chasing his into his mouth.

He groaned at her aggressiveness, then laughed. She felt the curve of his smile against her lips. He pulled back enough to gaze down at her, and she knew he would see his happiness mirrored in her face.

"How do you feel?" he asked again.

"Reborn."

His smile widened.

"How do you feel?" she returned the question.

He considered his answer for a minute, trailing his fingers through her hair, over the narrow line of her nose, down to her chin. The morning light glinted through his hair, giving it a golden luster. She ran her hands through it, as if she could capture the sunshine and hold it. "Unafraid," he answered, his voice husky and hushed. "For the first time in a long, long time, I feel unafraid."

"Make love to me," she said.

He bowed to kiss her, less playfully this time. His tongue moved purposefully past her teeth, seeking its partner, engaging in amorous combat. There was no fear in this kiss, just robust desire, certainty, a masculine possessiveness that ignited bright, dazzling responses in every part of her body. She slid her hands under his shirt once more, and he broke the kiss long enough to unbutton it. As he lowered his mouth to hers again, she eased the shirt over his shoulders and down his arms, baring his back to her eager hands.

His skin was smooth, meltingly warm. She explored the knots and ridges of his shoulders, the steel-hard muscles of his upper arms, the thick bones and sinews in his wrists. Her fingers found his and twined through them, and her hair spilled over their interlocked hands like a silken waterfall.

"*You* are the miracle," he whispered, sliding his mouth from her lips to her cheeks, to her chin, her throat. "You're the miracle that happened here."

That was an absurd notion, but she was too happy to argue. People weren't miracles. What occurred between two people could be miraculous, though. Love was a miracle.

Judd extricated his hands from hers and pulled the sweatshirt up, over her head. Naked to the waist, she closed her eyes as he glided his fingers down between her breasts, around one and then the other, skirting the sensitive skin. His touch was gentle, unhurried, lulling and exciting her at the same time. When at last his path reached the taut bud of her nipple, she let out a shaky sigh.

He filled his other hand with her other breast, and she opened her eyes to discover him above her, gazing down at her, his eyes making love to her as his hands did. He bowed and brushed his lips over hers, then kissed her again, deeply yet still slowly, only the slightest hint of urgency creeping into his movements.

Arousal filled her with the same strange mixture of languor and urgency. The pressure built slowly but inexorably, sending waves of sensation down from her lips to her breasts and then lower, to parts of her that Judd had yet to conquer.

Reading the delicious torment in her expression, he trailed his hands down to her waist to undo the tie on her sweatpants. He slid the pants down, off her legs and away.

She felt the chill of her nakedness for several seconds before he returned to her, sheltering her body with his. He had removed his jeans, as well, and she welcomed the sensation of his legs against hers, his hips poised above hers. Her hands toured his back to his buttocks, stroking, kneading, gliding forward. He raised himself to give her room, and she tightened her fingers around him, trembling with pleasure as he announced his own delight with a groan.

"Let me be under you," he murmured, then gasped as her thumb brushed a particularly sensitive spot.

She shook her head. She wanted to take his weight, to feel the full force of him, to let him lead. She wanted his power surging through her. A few bruises didn't matter.

He hesitated, giving her a chance to change her mind. She ran her palm the length of him, and he interpreted that as some sort of decision. Bringing his hand down between her legs, he slid his fingers between the damp folds of skin, discovering her own particularly sensitive spots and mastering them with deft, devastating strokes. Her body tensed, her nerve endings quivered; every sensation in her body focused on his fingertips, on the hollow inside her that waited, aching, for Judd.

She rocked her hips against his hand, moaning in glorious frustration as he probed deeper, increasing the tension, the desire, the crazed, mindless need. Her patience eroding, she guided him to herself, arching up as he surged, taking all of him.

He caught his breath; she caught her lower lip in her teeth. For a moment they lay motionless, joined together, savoring the unity, the merging of their spirits as well as their bodies.

Judd's eyes met hers in an equally expressive union. She gazed into their startling blue depths, perceiving the heat and hunger, the need and affection, the pleasure and pain, the knowledge of greater pleasure lurking just beyond their reach.

Then he moved, and she felt her flesh burn with renewed life. His thrusts were deep and powerful, each one taking a little more, giving a little more, carrying her a little further from herself, a little closer to him. His lips grazed her brow; his fingers wove through hers and pinned her hands against the mattress. The hair on his chest rubbed against her breasts, stimulating her nipples until they were tight and tingling.

She wrapped her legs around his hips, bringing him deeper. She saw the tendons in his neck stand out as his control began to fray. His thrusts became harder, more adamant; his eyes seemed to darken as the passionate demands of his body grew more imperative.

She responded with demands of her own. She arched higher, striving for more, more heat, more depth, more of Judd—until she could no longer contain herself. With a fierce lunge, he pushed her beyond her limits, splintering her soul into a million pieces, a million fiery, throbbing pulses. In an instant he was sharing her jubilation, living the miracle with her.

Emitting a breathless groan, he released her hands and wrapped his arms around her, rolling onto his side and pulling her against him. His mouth covered hers in a languid kiss; his hands roamed up and down her back in a soothing pattern. Alana slid one leg between his, provoking another guttural groan from him. She curled her fingers through his hair, holding his mouth to hers, drinking him in.

He rubbed his thigh against her, and her body contracted in an echo of bliss. Hearing her gasp, he flexed his thigh harder, higher, and her body erupted in a shimmering chain of spasms. When she cried out, he tightened his embrace, ushering her through the rapturous descent.

Her hands fisted at the back of his head, then unfurled as her body relaxed. She rested her head against his shoulder, relishing the strong, solid feel of him, the peace that drifted through her in the aftermath of such intense joy.

"I love you, Judd," she murmured, nestling as close to him as she could get without climbing inside his skin.

He said nothing. She instantly regretted having spoken her heart—and then she decided she didn't regret it. After the past few minutes—after the past six days—she couldn't lie to him. Whether she was ailing or well, bruised or luxuriating in the ecstasy of his lovemaking, her body couldn't lie. And whether she was arguing with him or sharing her most intimate hopes and fears, her heart couldn't lie.

Not even if speaking the truth made him run away.

He didn't run. He didn't recoil, didn't even loosen his hold on her. His fingers moved in lazy circles on her skin; his lips brushed the crown of her head. Perhaps he didn't love her; perhaps he couldn't. Perhaps his heart belonged to his girlfriend back in New York.

Miracles were hard to come by, though. You had to grab them where and when you found them, and treasure them for as long as you could, and harbor no regret once they were gone.

He brought his hand forward to her chin and tipped her head back until her eyes aligned with his. "This isn't the real world," he said quietly. "I believe in reality, Alana. But this...what we've lived through..." He sighed. "I don't know how it can be real."

"Because a miracle happened here?"

"Too many miracles."

"You don't have to believe them," she suggested. "You can just accept them."

"I don't know how." He looked pensive. The sky blue of his eyes was shadowed by storm clouds. "I just don't know how," he sighed, then leaned toward her and kissed her with a poignancy that filled her eyes with tears. He was being as honest with her as she'd been with him, and his honesty only made her love him more.

The air in the room had grown cool. Judd must have felt the drop in temperature, too. He sat up and looked past her at the stove. The fire was dying down.

He grabbed his jeans, pulled them on and stood. Alana watched sadly as he tended to the fire. There was coffee to be made, a basin to fill for the morning's water supply, things to be done. A day to be lived, if they were permitted to live it.

To be permitted to live was more than enough of a miracle, she tried to convince herself. Only a greedy person would dare to wish for more.

She noticed her clothes on a chair, where Judd had piled them yesterday. Bracing herself for her walk to the chair, she stood. Her legs wobbled under her. If Judd hadn't spun around and caught her under the arms, she might have collapsed. "Whoa," she gasped as he eased her back onto the cot.

"You've been through a lot," he reminded her.

Sure, she'd been through a lot. Crashes, chills, nightmares and the most excruciatingly tender lovemaking in the world. She was in love with a man who couldn't share her faith in love. Dizziness and weak knees seemed appropriate.

He brought her clothing to her, and she dressed while he turned his attention back to the firebox. The logs tumbled, snapped and hissed. The metal door squeaked and clanged. Eventually he had the fire blazing again.

It was only when he stopped banging around the stove that the cabin grew quiet enough for them to hear the sound: helicopter rotors. Distant but approaching. Growing louder. And louder.

Snatching his shirt from the chair, Judd raced to the door, swung it open and leaned out. The chugging noise of a helicopter engine blasted through the doorway. It slowed to an idle speed, and then the metallic static of a two-way radio resounded through the forest, followed by a tinny, amplified voice.

The words were garbled but the meaning was clear.

Judd stepped back inside and turned to Alana. "We're saved."

Chapter Twelve

She ought to have felt relieved, if not thrilled beyond words.

What she felt was betrayed.

The man in the khaki uniform, olive green parka and sturdy boots was going to take her away from this place, bring her home and hand her back her life.

Yet his presence in the cabin seemed liked a violation of the intimate, sheltering home she and Judd had shared. Suddenly they had a stranger in their midst, an invader. The static crackle of his walkie-talkie roiled the air as he summoned his colleague in the clearing. "We've got two survivors. Repeat, two ambulatory survivors, over."

Judd brought Alana her loafers and jacket. He sat beside her on the cot as she stepped into the shoes, then helped her on with her coat. She waited for him to admit that maybe he *did* believe, a little bit, or that magic might truly exist outside of toy wands and chemistry shows, or even that he would carry the memory of the past six days with him for the rest of his life. She searched his face for an indication that, as happy as he was to be rescued, he also felt a sense of loss.

His eyes remained blank, his emotions carefully shuttered. The nape of her neck tingled from the light brush of his fingertips when he lifted her hair out over the collar of her jacket; her body flushed with the recent memory of what those fingertips had felt like elsewhere on her body, loving her.

Certainly *her* eyes couldn't be blank. She had already told him she loved him, and as their gazes merged she sent him a frantic plea to tell her that the past few days meant something to him, something essential, something transcendent.

All he said was, "Let's go."

He helped her to her feet and she swayed against him, feeling light-headed and dazed. "She's been sick," Judd informed the rescue worker, tightening his arm around her to keep her from falling.

"We've got a stretcher in the chopper," the man said, lifting his walkie-talkie to his mouth.

"No." She stopped him. "I'm not an invalid. I want to walk out of here." She already felt defeated; to be carried out would be yet another defeat.

Judd refused to let go of her. His arm remained snug around her as they trudged slowly through the woods to the clearing, where a rescue helicopter was parked, its rotor turning slowly. Her legs felt rubbery, her feet too heavy to lift, but he kept her moving up the slope to the clearing through the dense snow.

In the clearing, a second rescue worker was surveying the wreckage, taking photographs. He turned at their approach and bounded through the snow to them.

"All right," he said briskly. "We're going to get you out of here. There are just the two of you, right?"

"Right," Judd answered. He had to shout to be heard over the drone of the helicopter engine. "I want you to take her straight to a hospital. Then you can come back for me."

She opened her mouth to object, but before she could speak one of the crew men was talking. "That won't be necessary. We can evacuate you both—"

"I have to go back," Judd explained. "I have to straighten up the cabin and collect my things. She needs immediate medical attention."

"Judd." She didn't want to leave without him. Medical attention wasn't anywhere near as important as having Judd with her on the flight off the mountain.

He turned her to face him. "You have to go," he said in a low, intense voice. She could scarcely hear him, but she felt his words like four quick blows to her soul.

"Why can't you come with me?"

He mulled over his answer. She saw a flash of emotion in his eyes—anguish, sorrow, remorse, she didn't know what—and then he resurrected his carefully wrought dispassion. "I can't leave the cabin a mess. It isn't ours. It belongs to someone."

It belonged to us, she wanted to cry. For a few crazy, perilous, awe-filled days it had been theirs.

"You have to go," Judd repeated, his hands gripping her shoulders even as his eyes grew colder and more distant. "You nearly died."

"But I didn't," she protested, thinking that if she left without him she *would* die.

Again he considered his words. She watched the sensual motion of his lips, the fleeting glint of heat once again sparking a pained blue light in his eyes before it burned out. Without speaking, he lifted her into his arms and carried her to the waiting helicopter. Evidently, if he couldn't argue with her, he'd overrule her with his superior strength.

She hated him for carrying her—yet all she wanted to do was cuddle closer to him, feel his arms locked around her, press her mouth to the warm hollow of his neck.

No use kissing him. No use pleading. Judd had already told her he didn't love her.

When he lowered her into the passenger seat, she looked away.

One of the rescue workers appeared at the open door by the controls. "Okay," he addressed her cheerfully. "I'm going to take you down the mountain. My partner's going to stay here with the gentleman. I'll send another chopper to get them."

Alana wanted to shout *no!* But it wouldn't matter. This was what Judd wanted. He was the magician; he was going to make her disappear.

Judd reached across her to fasten her seat belt. She watched his hands move gingerly over her abdomen. She wasn't sure if she was imagining the tremor in his fingers. Maybe he was just shivering from the cold.

But he hadn't been shivering when he'd clung to her shoulders, when he'd stared down into her eyes and told her she had to go. Not just for her sake, she understood, but for his.

She gazed up at him and she saw it again—the flare of emotion, burning briefly and then extinguished. In that fleeting glimmer of passion she saw the need he couldn't give voice to, couldn't admit to, couldn't believe. That was what he'd said—he didn't know how to believe.

The pilot climbed in beside her, strapped himself in, donned his headset and checked the controls. Judd smoothed the seat belt gently across Alana's hips, straightened up and brushed a long black tendril from her cheek. Then he turned, closed the door and stood with the other rescue worker, out of range of the churning rotor.

The helicopter rose off the ground, hovered, then rose higher. Alana looked down through the window without seeing the clearing, the plane's snow-covered remains, the trees, the thread of smoke rising from the chimney of the hunter's cabin. All she saw was Judd, returning her steady, desperate gaze until he was too small to make out. The helicopter banked southward and Alana closed her eyes.

"I'm going to take you straight down to Boston," the pilot told her after he'd radioed his plans to an unseen voice somewhere on the ground.

"Oh." What did she care where he took her?

"Quite an experience, wasn't it? We've been searching for you folks for six days."

"You flew right over us," she told him. "At least three or four times. You flew directly over us, and we waved and shouted and tied a blanket to the wreckage..."

The pilot gave her a puzzled look. "I don't think so. The air traffic controller had the wrong coordinates for you when you went down. We've been searching the mountains near the Maine border, a good eighty miles east of where you actually were. After a couple of days, we decided he must have located you incorrectly, and we expanded the search area." The pilot shook his head. "That controller's in big trouble."

Alana shuddered. She had seen the rescue helicopters flying overhead. Judd had seen them. They had beamed their searchlights at the wreckage. She hadn't dreamed it all, had she?

"Cold?" the pilot asked. "There's a blanket in back. I should have gotten it for you before we took off."

She would be cold for the rest of her life. "I'm fine," she said.

"I'll tell you, it's a miracle you two survived for so long. No other way to call it. It was a miracle."

Perhaps, she thought, *if you believed in miracles.* Judd didn't, though, and she was no longer certain she believed in anything.

An oppressive chill settled over her, one from which the blanket in the back wouldn't have protected her. Sighing, she shoved her hands into the pockets of her jacket. Her left hand felt her gloves, and her right felt a carved wooden shape.

Her fingers traced the right angles, the point, the knob. The engraved Hebrew letters. *Nes gadol haya po. A miracle happened here.*

She didn't remember putting the dreidel in her pocket. Maybe Judd had tucked it there. Or maybe it didn't exist; maybe she was dreaming that it was there, imagining she could feel it.

Maybe it didn't matter what was real, what was magic, what were dreams. Maybe she *hadn't* survived.

Maybe this rescue was just another dream.

THE HELICOPTER delivered her to Hanscom Air Force Base, near Boston, where an ambulance and a squadron of newspaper reporters awaited her. Mainly to avoid talking to the reporters, Alana let herself be strapped to a stretcher and wheeled to the ambulance.

Her parents were at the hospital when she was brought in. Her father was weeping openly; her mother, while showing evidence—damp cheeks and bloodshot eyes—of a recent crying jag, was too busy ordering everyone around to give in to tears. "No reporters now!" she shouted to the people swarming around Alana. "Leave my daughter alone! Come on, come on, get a doctor over here! Alana, baby, we love you so much..."

There was a swift ride down a long, well-lit corridor. Someone took her blood pressure. Someone else pulled off her shoes. A curtain was yanked shut, metal loops ringing against a metal curtain rod. Through the curtain she could hear her mother issuing more commands and her father murmuring, "Our baby's back. Thank God, our baby's back."

She was examined from her scalp to her toenails. The staff cleaned out the gash on her forehead, gave her a tetanus shot, drew blood, and X-rayed her hip and shoulder. To her great relief, not one doctor, nurse or orderly asked her about what her life on the mountain had been like, what she'd done, how she and Judd had kept each other alive.

"I want a shower," she said once the doctors were done poking and prodding her and she was brought upstairs to a private room. "A hot shower, with shampoo."

Although she had to sit on a stool in the tiny shower stall, with a nurse posted right outside the curtain in case she fell, the shower was heavenly. For the first time in nearly a week she got to wash in water that hadn't entered her life in the form of snow. She lathered her hair and stared at the thick, fragrant foam in her hands in amazement. Even the starchy institutional towels felt wonderful against her skin.

Clad in a soft hospital gown, she was sent back to the sterile room and tucked into bed, her forehead freshly bandaged and her arm hooked up to an intravenous bottle. An energetic young doctor told her that, while the cut on her forehead might have benefited from a couple of sutures, she wouldn't be badly scarred. Her pelvic bone, he reported, had been chipped. It was the sort of injury that might enable her to predict changes in the weather for the rest of her life, but it wouldn't slow her down.

Her parents joined her in the small room and
something shut down inside her. She loved her parents, and she'd missed them terribly during her ordeal. But if she couldn't be with Judd, she didn't want
to be with anyone.

Her parents accepted her remoteness as a natural
reaction to what she'd been through. Her father pulled
up a chair beside the bed, held her hand and said
nothing. Her mother stood vigil near the door, issuing more orders to any hospital employee who happened by.

When one of her brothers arrived, a nurse tried to
bar him from the room, reciting hospital regulations
about how only two visitors were allowed at a time.
"This isn't a visitor," Alana's mother argued, grabbing Kenny's arm and dragging him through the
doorway, past the nurse. "This is her brother."

"I've been in meetings all morning," Kenny told
Alana as he set a bouquet of flowers on the table beside her and sat on the edge of her bed. "When Mom
called and said you were found—it was incredible.
Don't do this to us again, okay?"

"I'll try not to."

"You look beautiful."

"I look like hell."

"You're alive, Lannie. That's as beautiful as it
gets."

His eyes filled with tears, and she glanced away. Her
mother and father were still weepy, too. But her own
eyes remained resolutely dry. She didn't know why she
couldn't cry the way her loved ones could. Maybe she
was too tired. Or maybe it was just that something in-

side her—the part of her that believed and felt things and wept—had died.

Had she actually begun that day in the mountains of New Hampshire? Had she actually begun it in Judd Singer's arms?

Judd. Thinking about him made the place inside her that used to be alive ache in a phantom memory of what love and pain felt like. *Judd.* He was gone. To be rescued meant to be torn from him. To be found meant to be lost forever.

This was reality, she kept telling herself. Reality was a clean, bright room at Beth Israel Hospital in Boston. It was electrical lights and radiators, crisp linens and the muffled sound of a television set in a neighboring room. It was her family.

Forget the mountain, she ordered herself. *Forget the man. Forget the miracles.*

A candle had once burned in her soul, shedding its light upon her. Real life had blown it out in a single puff.

THE PHONE rang again.

Thank goodness for answering machines, he thought, remaining in his leather easy chair as the machine picked up what had to be the fiftieth phone call he received since he had gotten home an hour ago. "Singer?" a voice emerged through the speaker. "It's Pete. I just got off the phone with your office, and they said you're back from the dead. Hey, man, that's great! Welcome to the world! Listen, I'm around if you want to talk, and if you're up for a game of squash I'll rearrange my life. Seriously, I'm real glad you're back. I missed you, buddy. Couldn't find anyone who can return my serve as well as you. Give me a call.'' Disconnected, the machine went silent.

Judd sighed and rested his head against the leather upholstery. On the table to his left sat the pile of mail his neighbors had dutifully removed from his mailbox in the lobby every day of his absence. He had sorted through most of it—a few bills, a lot of Christmas cards from people hoping to do business with him, a lot of circulars advertising the seasonal sales.

At his right hand was a glass of Chivas, neat—twelve-years-old, properly aged, nothing like the rotgut he'd drunk with Alana.

Behind him was an hour-long visit with his physician, who had declared him remarkably fit. Ahead of him was...

He didn't know.

The picture window across the room turned from blue to black. He had left the light on in the kitchen, so the living room wasn't completely dark. He wasn't yet ready to turn on the lamp at his elbow.

He took a long sip of Scotch, then lowered the glass to the end table. The phone rang again. He didn't move.

''Mr. Singer? This is John Randolph from *New York* magazine. I'd like to do an interview with you, if we can set something up. I think you've got a terrific story to tell, and I can assure you I'll tell it with taste. I'd like to discuss terms with you. Please telephone me....''

New York magazine. He'd already heard from the *Times*, *USA Today*, *People*, and two supermarket tabloids. Also an independent producer from Hollywood who wanted to buy the rights to a made-for-TV film about the crash. "High quality," the producer had gushed. "A-list casting. I plan to be in touch with Miss Halpern, as well."

Alana.

He couldn't get a phone message without thinking of her. He couldn't take a drink of Scotch without thinking of her. He couldn't close his eyes without seeing her, or open them without wanting her.

It wasn't supposed to be like this.

He had said goodbye to her. Not in so many words, but his eyes had said it. The final look they exchanged had said it.

She had gone back to Boston and he had gone back to the cabin with the man from the chopper. There, he'd packed his duffel bag, cleaned up the cabin and wrote the cabin's unknown owner a check for five hundred dollars.

Several hours later he was in a cab, cruising from La Guardia Airport into Manhattan. His first stop was his office, where he was welcomed like a conquering hero. His small, frenzied staff gathered around him, shrieking and hugging him. They deluged him with questions he was in no mood to answer. Earl Bingham raced to the corner gourmet shop for hot bagels and fresh-ground coffee; Lynn Wentworth updated him on all the sales figures for the week; Melissa, his trusty secretary, told him enough to reassure him that the Magic Shops had made it through their leaderless days with panache—"Not to be crass, Judd, but the free publicity from your disappearance really boosted sales in certain markets.''

By the time Earl had returned, Judd couldn't bear another minute in the office. He promised to catch up on his work tomorrow, and bolted.

He couldn't understand it. He enjoyed his job and his colleagues. He thrived on the challenges, took an enormous interest in details, and never turned down a fresh bagel.

But that was before. This was after. Everything was different.

The telephone rang, and the machine clicked on: "Judd, it's Dad again." Judd had spoken with his parents several times, the first call from a borrowed office at the Laconia airport where the rescue helicopter had brought him. "Mom and I were talking about it some more, and we aren't sure you should come here. We'll come to New York. We're concerned about your getting on an airplane so soon after... Well. We want to see you. Here or there. Call us when you feel up to it, and we'll discuss it some more.''

He'd ridden in an airplane, a turboprop not much larger than the Beechcraft, from Laconia to New York without any qualms. He hadn't panicked, hadn't suffered any flashbacks. He was sure he could handle a flight to Boise without undue anxiety.

Except that every time he thought of leaving New York his vision pointed north, not west. North and east to Boston.

Was she all right? Regaining her strength? Basking in the warmth of her family?

Did she miss him as much as he missed her?

She'd been the one to talk about love. But that was because she and Judd had just made love. She had wanted to put into words what they'd expressed with their bodies.

It had no bearing on *this*, though, the two-hundred-fifty miles that separated his life from hers. Whatever distorted emotions they'd experienced in that hot-house, cold-cabin environment didn't pertain to the real world.

In the real world he was an entrepreneur, living in a modern one-bedroom co-op overlooking the East River, and she was an artist living in a loft across the Charles River from Boston. They couldn't go back to what they'd been during their days in the wilderness. That was history. They had to move forward.

To what?

He couldn't love her. She believed in miracles, rituals, sentimentality. He believed in reality.

So why had he kept that one drawing?

He drained his glass and went into the bedroom. From the duffel bag he pulled out the drawing—the one of him and Alana seated across the table from each other with her Hanukkah candle burning between them. They were on the verge of breaking into the light. Their hands lay in the bright circle but their faces remained in shadow, longing for illumination but afraid to get too close to it, too close to each other.

At the time he'd slipped the drawing into his bag, he had told himself he intended to mail it to her. She had said she wanted to show it to her children someday. He could mail it to her in care of Neeley, Henderson, just stick it in an envelope with a little note, wishing her well.

A little note, telling her he was thinking about her.

A little note telling her he couldn't *stop* thinking about her.

He cursed, tossed the drawing onto his dresser and left the room. This wasn't how it was supposed to happen. He was supposed to be trying to get back to normal.

His phone was ringing. He walked into the kitchen, refilled his glass and listened as a reporter from New York *Newsday* requested an interview "at your convenience." When the reporter hung up, the machine clicked off.

Judd lifted the receiver and dialed. Susan answered on the second ring. "Hello?"

"Hello, Susan."

"Judd? Oh, my God! Judd?"

"Yes." He took a bracing sip of Scotch.

"Where are you?"

"In my apartment." He glanced at the clock built into the wall-unit oven. Six-fifteen. "Can I see you?"

"Now?" He heard a trilling, slightly nervous laugh. "Oh, God, Judd! You've really taken me by surprise. I talked to your secretary first thing this morning—I've been calling every morning. She never said—"

"She didn't know first thing this morning. I just got back to the city a few hours ago."

"A few hours! Why didn't you call me right away?"

"I've been busy." That sounded pretty lame, even if it was the truth. "I went straight to the doctor—"

"Oh, no. Tell me you're all right, Judd."

"I'm all right. Really. I'm in excellent health. I wanted to hear him say it, and he did."

"Thank God."

"Yeah." He drummed his fingers against the butcher-block counter. Why had it been so easy to be honest with Alana—even when he knew his honesty might hurt her? His honesty might hurt Susan, too, but he saw no way around it. "I'd like to see you."

"Oh, Judd, I wish you'd called earlier. I'm just on my way out. I'm supposed to meet Chet Tillinghast and his sister for dinner over near Columbus Circle. But say, why don't you join us? Chet and Bibi won't mind."

"No."

"I'm sorry. You've probably been through all sorts of terrible things, and here I am babbling about going out to dinner. Look—I can't phone them, since they're going to the restaurant straight from work, but I can meet them there and beg off for dinner, and then we could get together, or—you must be exhausted. Why don't I pick up some take-out and—"

"No." He hadn't been exhausted until he called her. Had their social life always been this fraught with fussy arrangements and schedules?

He hadn't intended to sound blunt, but apparently he did. "Judd. I'm trying to be accommodating. It's not as if I wasn't worried half to death about you, but I'm afraid I didn't throw out my calendar and crawl into a hole."

"That's okay," he said, his tone softening. "I want to talk to you Susan. I thought it would be better if we talked in person, but if you can't—"

"I can try. Let me—"

"Susan." He took a swallow of Scotch, then sighed. "I've . . . I've changed."

She fell silent for a minute. "Changed?"

"I'm not the same person I was when I got on that plane a week ago. I wish to God I was, but I'm not."

"What happened? Were you hurt? You just said the doctor—"

"I wasn't hurt. But . . . I've changed."

"Because you faced death?"

"Because I faced love." It was out. He'd said it. What he'd learned from Alana—honesty, faith, love— couldn't be unlearned.

"I'm confused. Are you in love with someone?"

"No. I don't know. I . . ." He sighed again. He couldn't possibly explain something he himself didn't understand and didn't want, but there it was. "Miracles happened, Susan. Magic happened. I witnessed it. I was a part of it. There was this kerosene lamp that wouldn't go out. Day after day, it had only a drop of fuel in it, yet it refused to burn out. And there was a woodpile that kept replenishing itself—"

"Judd." She sounded very solemn now, almost grave. "Judd, did you discuss this with your doctor?"

"No."

"Before you talk to anyone else, maybe you ought to talk to someone who's trained in this sort of thing."

"Who? A rabbi?"

A long pause, and then she said, "I was thinking of a psychologist."

She thought he was insane. A week ago he might have agreed with her. "I'm trying to tell you, Susan—you don't come out of something like this the way you went into it. I don't know if I'm better or worse because of what I've gone through, but I can't alter the truth. It happened, and it changed me."

He listened to dead air on the wire. At last she spoke. "I think you have some things to work out on your own."

"Yes."

"And . . . it might be better for both of us if I'm not a part of it."

"Yes."

"Well, then." Another long pause. "I'd better go."

"I'm sorry, Susan. We should have talked about this face-to-face."

"No, it's all right. I'd better go."

"Take care of yourself."

"You, too." She hung up.

He lowered the phone into the cradle, stared at it a long minute and then walked back into the living room. He had left his glass in the kitchen, but he decided not to go back for it. He didn't want to get drunk. He needed his mind as clear as it could be.

Everything he'd admitted to Susan had been the truth. He didn't know if he was in love. Didn't know if he was better or worse because of what he'd endured. All he knew was that he wasn't the same man he used to be.

He left the lamps off. He had spent enough recent evenings in near darkness lately to have gotten accustomed to it.

He strolled to the wide picture window and looked out. Lights in the residential towers on Roosevelt Island across the river twinkled. Some of the terraces had been strung with colorful Christmas bulbs; they flashed and sparkled, lending the vista a playful, almost gaudy air.

The view wasn't as spectacular as what he'd seen standing in the clearing near the cabin. The White Mountains didn't need multicolored Christmas lights to dazzle a human being; they had a night sky filled with shining stars and a silver moon.

Light, Judd acknowledged, took different forms at different times. Sometimes it was moon and stars, sometimes the electric lights of civilized people turning their private little dwellings into homes. Sometimes it was a candle flickering on a table. Sometimes it was the glow in a lover's eyes.

Light, he contemplated, gazing at the world outside his window. When you were surrounded by darkness, light was the miracle.

Chapter Thirteen

Everyone was waiting for her.

While she'd bathed, Alana had heard the cheery sounds of the guests arriving downstairs at her parents' house for the celebration of Hanukkah's last night. She had to go down soon.

She ran the brush through her hair one last time and dressed in the brown velvet jumper and ivory silk blouse that her mother had picked up from her apartment yesterday when Alana had been discharged from the hospital.

While her mother had been in Cambridge, Alana had sat in a special lounge at the hospital and met with reporters hankering for the story of the courageous young lady pilot who'd survived a plane crash and six days in the snowy wilderness of New Hampshire's White Mountains. She had answered their questions calmly and stoically, all the while imagining that Judd was enduring equally tedious interviews in New York—and reminding herself she wasn't supposed to care.

Too many times since her rescue she had wondered whether everything—the crash, Judd, the profound love she felt for him—had been a dream. But she knew it was all real. She had proof: the dreidel. Right now it was tucked into the side pocket of her jumper. Silly as it was, she needed it with her, assuring her that miracles could happen anywhere and everywhere if only she believed.

If only she believed. She didn't believe, not anymore. She was rescued, she was safe, and there was nothing more to believe in.

She heard a tap on her door and it swung wide as her six-year-old niece, Emily, pranced in. "Hey, Aunt Alana, Gramma said to tell you to come down because almost everybody's here and it's going to be sundown soon and they want you there when they light the menorah."

To celebrate the safe and sound return of her daughter, Alana's mother had invited everyone back to the house for the final night of Hanukkah. Countless neighbors had also stopped by to wish her well; the kitchen table was heaped high with cookies, flowers and bottles of wine, all for her.

And meanwhile, she had cloistered herself in the room that had been hers as a girl, trying her damnedest to pretend she was delighted when all she wanted was to go home to her own apartment, curl up under the blankets in her bed, and try to figure out a way to live the rest of her life without Judd.

Through the open door she heard the din of people talking and laughing downstairs in the living room.

Emily took her hand. She managed a feeble smile for her niece, and they left the room together.

The living room wasn't that crowded, but it seemed jam-packed to Alana. After six days of seeing no one but Judd, she hadn't yet gotten used to being among swarms of people.

Aunt Sylvie rushed to her side and kissed her cheek. "We love you, sweetheart," she said. "Come in, come sit on the sofa. Would you like something to drink?"

"No, thank you."

Her brother Richard materialized by her side and ushered her to the overstuffed couch. Uncle Myron took one of her hands in both of his and kissed her knuckles. Richard's wife, Ellen, plopped herself onto the cushion next to Alana and handed her the baby. "Look, Michael—it's Auntie Alana!" Ellen cooed, spreading a clean cloth diaper across Alana's lap to protect her skirt.

Dressed in dapper corduroy overalls, his fine dark hair curling away from his scalp and his hands reaching for Alana's chin, Michael gave her a bright, toothless smile. He smelled like baby powder; his chubby cheeks dimpled as he swiped at her with his adorably clumsy arms. "He recognizes me," Alana said, surprised.

"Of course he does," Ellen assured her. "Why shouldn't he?"

Because I'm not myself anymore, she almost answered.

She balanced the baby on her knees. Behind him she could see the beautiful brass menorah displayed on a table near the window so its beauty could be shared

with the world outside. Eight white candles were fit-
ted into the eight level holders, with the ninth, the
shammas, rising above them. "Look, Michael—look
at the pretty candles."

Michael just giggled and gurgled and grabbed a
fistful of her hair.

She almost cried. Almost laughed. She felt nothing
for herself, but for Michael, this precious little baby,
her emotions twitched to life.

Alana's mother, trailed by Aunt Edith and Aunt
Sylvie, trooped in from the kitchen. "It's time to light
the menorah," her father announced, setting down the
bottle of wine he had been opening.

Her parents' guests gravitated toward the table by
the window; conversations petered out and a respect-
ful hush descended on the room.

"Alana," her mother called to her. "Would you like
to light the candles?"

Ellen lifted the baby off Alana's lap. Alana swallowed, thinking of the holiday candles she had already lit that year, the fat, waxy stubs jammed into an
ashtray in a chilly, dark shack perched on a snowy,
forested mountain. "No," she answered. "Let the
children do it."

Her niece and nephew leaped forward exuberantly.
Alana's father touched a burning match to the *shammas,* then handed it first to Emily and then to her
brother Adam as they brought its flame to the eight
waiting candles. Her parents recited the prayers together, their voices winding around each other in a
melodious counterpoint.

The Hebrew words sounded strange yet familiar to Alana. She remembered bits and pieces, deeply buried meanings. "... These lights are sacred," her father recited, reaching the end of the final prayer, "and we shall make no use of them, but simply look at them and give thanks to God for His miracles, His deliverances and His wonders."

"Amen," chorused Alana's family.

A voice began to sing the Hanukkah song, soft and bright. Other guests joined in.

One for each night they shed a sweet light, to remind us of days long ago...

The words of the song coiled through her, triggering pangs of memory, of grief, of the night she had sung this song for Judd, and danced with him, and leaned against him, finding her strength in his. This song would always remind her of those days, so recent yet seemingly a lifetime ago.

The room crowded her, closed in on her. The air was too still, too stifling. She had to get out.

She sidled over to her brother Kenny and whispered, "Can I borrow your car?"

He frowned.

"Please. I've got to get away for a while."

"But what about dinner? What about Hanukkah?"

"Please, Kenny—I have to do this." She didn't know *why* she had to. Maybe it was like the morning after the blizzard, when she'd had to leave the cabin even though that compulsion to get out had nearly cost her her life.

Her brother seemed to recognize her need. He dug into his pocket and pulled out his keys. "Will you be back in time for dinner?"

"Tell Mom and Dad not to wait," she said. "I'll be back when I can."

Stepping outside into the crystal night air made her feel better, stronger. She was taking charge, taking steps, doing something. A strict interpretation of Jewish law would have barred her from driving a car after sundown on a holiday—but even the strictest interpretation allowed a person to break a rule if she felt her life was at stake.

At that moment, as she moved in steady strides down the snow-trimmed sidewalk to her brother's car, Alana felt her life was as much at stake as it had been during her six days in the wilderness. She had survived—but she wouldn't be fully alive until she had once again taken charge of her destiny.

She settled behind the wheel and a wave of fear racked her. The car in no way resembled an airplane cockpit, she had to remind herself. "I'm not going to fall out of the sky," she said aloud. "I'm not going to crash."

Even so, her heart raced as she twisted the key in the ignition.

She drove slowly through the quiet streets of her parents' neighborhood, feeling more and more confident with each mile. She cruised onto Beacon Street, then north over the Charles River and finally into Cambridge.

Why hadn't she come home sooner? She'd been rescued two days ago, but she hadn't returned to her apartment until now. Maybe she had subconsciously wanted to avoid the place; coming home meant that her life was truly going to continue. And Judd wasn't going to be in it.

Forget him, a voice inside her cautioned. *He's gone. You're going to have to keep going without him. Accept the reality of it.*

She didn't accept the reality. She couldn't. She had walked out on her parents' party, their Festival of Lights. She had driven away from safety, away from the candles and the warmth and into the darkness— because she couldn't accept that particular reality.

She ought to have been afraid, but she wasn't. She felt as if she were flying again, breaking free, heading off into the eternal sky. Maybe she *would* crash—but she wasn't afraid.

She saw Judd.

He was standing by the front door of the converted Victorian house where she lived. His hair was tawny, streaked with blond, neatly combed. His jaw was shaved smooth. The collar of his long cashmere coat was turned up around his neck. He looked so... groomed.

She felt sparks of sensation inside her, twinges, the emotional anesthesia wearing off and her spirit awakening. She parked her brother's car and walked up the sidewalk to the house.

To Judd.

"I don't know why I'm here," he said.

He was there because something had lured him there, just as something had lured her away from her family. It had drawn her to her home, to her life, just as a clearing in the woods had drawn her to land her crippled plane in its cushion of snow.

Judd didn't believe in magic, but she did. "You're here," she told him, "because you had to come. And I'm here because I had to come."

He nodded. His eyes glowed with bemusement and something more: relief. Desire. A need for her as imperative as her need for him.

She was in his arms before she could halt herself. He held her close, his lips gliding over her brow, over the healing gash above her left eye, over her lids, to the tip of her nose. When at last his mouth came down on hers, she felt weak from the sudden, total return of sensation to every part of her body, every square inch of her soul.

"Come inside," she said when at last his lips released hers.

They didn't speak as she unlocked the front door and led him up the narrow stairs to her attic apartment. Stepping inside her living room, seeing the painting she'd been working on before the crash, the bright, riotous streaks of color soaring across the canvas, was all the proof she needed that she was still alive, still Alana Halpern, the painter, the artist, the woman she'd been a week ago.

She felt Judd behind her, resting his hands on her shoulders and gazing about the studio. Everywhere there were shelves with paint, cans of solvent, empty jars and rows of brushes. A paint-spattered drop cloth lay crumpled in a corner.

"We have to talk," he said. His hands moved on her in a gentle massage, his fingers relearning the shape of her shoulders through the soft velvet of her jumper. It dawned on her that she had forgotten to put on a coat before she left her parents' house—and that outside, in the nippy December evening, she hadn't even felt the cold.

He moved his fingers farther down her arms, pulling her back against him. Bowing, he touched a kiss to her earlobe.

If she had been warm before, she was warmer now. Infinitely warmer.

She spun around and linked her hands behind his neck. His mouth took hers again, hungrily, greedily, his tongue seeking and surging, conquering. His voice echoed inside her brain: *We have to talk.* But he had never been a talkative man, and at the moment, there were other things they had to do.

She wedged her fingers under the collar of his coat and along his shoulders, easing the fine, smooth cashmere down his arms. The coat fell to the floor, but he didn't bother to pick it up. Instead, he gathered fistfuls of velvet, hiking up her jumper and lifting it over her head.

She had a comfortable double bed in the next room, less than twenty-five feet away. Yet she couldn't stop kissing him, couldn't stop tugging at the buttons of his shirt, at his belt, at the fly of his trousers. He stripped off her clothes as she stripped off his, and all the while their mouths remained fused, drinking each other in, devouring each other.

When they were both finally naked, he pulled back and drew in a ragged breath. He was already hard, and she slid her hands eagerly over him, making him harder. He groaned in satisfaction and protest, pushing against her palms as he ran his hands down her back, up her sides to her breasts and down again, across her belly and lower, to her thighs, to the welcoming dampness between her legs. "I can't..." he whispered, skimming her hips to her bottom and angling her to him.

"Can't what?"

"Can't wait. I need you, Alana. Oh, God—I need you." He pulled her to himself, pressing his length into her, filling her.

She gasped, lifted her hands to his shoulders and clutched him tightly to keep from falling. He backed her against the wall, then began to move, holding her high against him, thrusting deeper and deeper until her entire body felt touched by him, inhabited by his heat. She dug her fingers into the taut muscles of his upper back, opened her mouth to his ferocious kisses, savored the harsh friction of his chest hair against her inflamed nipples. Lifting her higher, he cupped his hands under her, taking her full weight as he took all of her.

She felt the tension increase inside her, the stretching, seething, twisting crescendo of it until her body could withstand no more. With a moan, she gave herself over to it, let it consume her, let it pound through her in devastatingly sweet tremors of love. Only when she let her head sink against Judd's shoulder did he let go, pinning her to the wall with a final, overpowering thrust.

A long minute went by, punctuated by his rough, rasping breath and hers. Gradually she became aware of his fingers digging into the soft flesh of her bottom, his palms cupping her, his chest crushing her breasts every time he inhaled. She became aware of the sweat misting his broad, strong back, the pressure of his belly against hers, his lips against her temple.

"I have a bed," she said belatedly.

He laughed. His body slackened and slid from hers, and he eased her to her feet. Even though she wasn't about to fall, she held onto him because he felt so good.

He ran his hands up her sides to her face, stroking her cheeks, brushing back her hair, studying her. "How are you?" he asked.

She had been miserable. At the moment she felt magnificent. But whatever Judd had come to Cambridge to say to her might change how she was. "I don't know," she answered honestly.

"I couldn't stay away," he confessed. "I tried to, Alana. I rented a car and drove up to Boston, thinking I was going to meet with Mark Neeley. But I came here instead. I couldn't seem to stop myself."

"I know." That was exactly the way she'd felt when she'd left her parents' house less than a half hour ago. She couldn't stop herself.

"I wanted to give you something."

"You did," she said, smiling as she slid her hands boldly down the sleekly muscled surface of his abdomen to the nest of hair below.

He returned her smile, but his eyes remained solemn. Reluctantly, he nudged her hands away and took a step back. His gaze journeyed to the unfinished canvas against the wall and then returned to her.

His eyes were a bottomless blue. Cerulean. Wedgwood. She could gather her paints right now and try to mix the color on a palette. But she would never be able to make a blue as beautiful.

As her body cooled, she collected her wits. What had happened in the past few minutes was a burst of magic, she told herself. Now they had to be realistic again.

"You're going to leave," she said with a sudden, piercing awareness.

He turned back to her. "Why do you say that?"

"You always run away. It's what you do, Judd. It's what you did on the mountain. You wouldn't even leave with me. You just ran away."

"You're right." He scooped his coat off the floor and draped it around her shoulders. He walked her to the couch, retrieving his trousers along the way. Once he'd donned them, he sat and pulled her down beside him.

She knew she shouldn't say anything more, but she couldn't help herself. She hadn't hesitated to speak her mind on the mountain, and she didn't now. "You don't want me in your life," she said simply. "I haven't heard a word from you since we're back. I figured you were glad to be rid of me—"

He arched his arm around her, holding her so her head rested against his shoulder. "No, Alana. I wasn't glad."

"It was what you wanted."

"I didn't know what I wanted." He stroked his fingers through her hair in a lulling pattern. "All I knew was that something was wrong, something was missing." He lapsed into thought. "You're right. I did run away when we were rescued. I wanted to resume my normal life. I wanted to pick up where I left off."

She hadn't even tried to resume her normal life. She'd hidden from it—until the moment she'd gotten into her brother's car and driven to Cambridge. She had known, deep in her heart, that after what she'd been through, after the love and trust and faith she'd experienced, she could never pick up where she'd left off.

He clasped her hand in his, stroking his thumb over her fingers. "I can't keep running away, Alana. I can't pretend I don't believe in miracles. Not when I've lived them."

"You don't believe in miracles. You believe in reality."

"I'm realistic enough to know a miracle when I see one. And I'm smart enough to know when to stop running." He cupped his free hand under her chin and turned her face so he could see it. "I don't have your faith, Alana. And it's not easy to accept magic when everything you've ever known tells you there's no such thing. But we never ran out of wood on that mountain. We never ran out of kerosene, or food, or life. We should have, but we didn't." He grazed her forehead with his lips. "They were all miracles, Alana. But you are the greatest miracle I know. I love you."

The tears that before had threatened now spilled over, hot against her cheeks. She pulled her hand from his and covered her eyes.

Oh, God, it hurt. After so many days of emotional numbness, she was deluged by sensation. She felt pain, want, need, yearning. Joy and the fear of having that joy snatched away from her.

"And here I thought you'd be happy," he said.

"Oh, Judd…" She let out a tremulous sigh. "What about your girlfriend in New York?"

He shook his head. "She was never a girlfriend. Just a woman I socialized with. We weren't in love."

"But you told me—"

"I left you with certain misconceptions," he conceded. "I suppose it was just another way of running from you." He skimmed his thumbs across her cheeks, wiping away the moisture. Then he took her hand again, enveloping it in his. "I thought about flying to Idaho to visit my parents—they've been so worried about me. But I had to come here. I had to see you. And when I did…" He leaned toward her and brushed her lips with his. "I guess I got a little carried away. I didn't realize what seeing you would do to me."

"I missed you, too," she said with a gentle smile.

They kissed again, a deeper, longer kiss. He had said he loved her, and more than she'd ever believed anything in her life, she wanted to believe this: that he was here. That he would stay. That the miracle of love would be theirs forever.

Leaning back, he reached under her breast, searching for the inner pocket of his coat. He pulled out a folded sheet of paper. "This is yours. I told myself that was why I came—to give it to you."

Mystified, she took the paper and unfolded it. It was the drawing she had done the first night of Hanukkah, of her and Judd hovering at the edge of the candle's glow.

"I took it with me when I left the cabin," he told her. "You said you wanted to show it to your children someday. I was going to mail it to you, but..." He sighed. "I don't want to part with it. But it's yours, so I guess I have to."

"Judd—"

"You have to keep it. Someday you *will* have children to share your holiday rituals with. The continuum, wasn't that how you described it? The continuum. That's what that drawing is about."

"No," she argued. "It's about you and me." She slid out of his coat, out of his arms, and darted across the room to the mound of brown velvet lying on the floor. From the side pocket she removed the dreidel. "This is about you and me, too," she said, returning to the couch. "I don't want to part with it, either."

"We'll keep them together," he promised, bringing his arms around her. Instead of kissing her he only gazed at her. "You told me once that you loved me."

"Yes."

"Do you still?"

"I tried to stop, but I couldn't."

"I guess that's another miracle."

"No," she said, resting her hands on his shoulders. "It's just reality."

He kissed her then. His mouth matched hers, his tongue merged with hers, his arms held her with a strength born of love, faith, commitment and acceptance.

"I meant what I said before," he murmured, his voice husky in the aftermath of the kiss. "You should have children to share your life with. Our children. I want us to be a family."

"Yes," she whispered. She knew what he was asking, and her heart knew the only answer. "Yes."

They sat together, their arms around each other, their bodies unwinding peacefully on the cozy couch. Alana had neglected to turn on the lamps when they entered the apartment, but flickers of light came through the windows from the streetlights, from the headlights of cars, from the bright porch light on the house across the street.

Alana thought of the menorah at her parents' house, the lovely white candles, the dancing flames. Here, in her home, in Judd's arms, contentment and peace lit her soul like a row of burning candles. Warm and luminous, the light that blazed inside her spoke of love and magic, of miracles past and of miracles yet to come.

HAPPY VALENTINE'S DAY

James Rafferty had only forty-eight hours, and he wanted to make the most of them.... Helen Emerson had never had a Valentine's Day like this before!

Celebrate this special day for lovers, with a very special book from American Romance!

#473   ONE MORE VALENTINE
by Anne Stuart

Next month, Anne Stuart and American Romance have a delightful Valentine's Day surprise in store just for you. All the passion, drama—even a touch of mystery—you expect from this award-winning author.

Don't miss American Romance
#473   ONE MORE VALENTINE!

Also look for Anne Stuart's short story, "Saints Alive," in Harlequin's MY VALENTINE 1993 collection.

HARLEQUIN®
Temptation®
Rebels & Rogues

Jared: He'd had the courage to fight in Vietnam. But did he have the courage to fight for the woman he loved?

THE SOLDIER OF FORTUNE
By Kelly Street
Temptation #421, December

All men are not created equal. Some are rough around the edges. Tough-minded but tenderhearted. Incredibly sexy. The tempting fulfillment of every woman's fantasy.

When it's time to fight for what they believe in, to win that special woman, our Rebels and Rogues are heroes at heart. Twelve Rebels and Rogues, one each month in 1992, only from Harlequin Temptation.

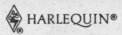

my Valentine 1993

The most romantic day of the year is here! Escape into the exquisite world of love with MY VALENTINE 1993. What better way to celebrate Valentine's Day than with this very romantic, sensuous collection of four original short stories, written by some of Harlequin's most popular authors.

**ANNE STUART
JUDITH ARNOLD
ANNE McALLISTER
LINDA RANDALL WISDOM**

**THIS VALENTINE'S DAY, DISCOVER ROMANCE
WITH MY VALENTINE 1993**

Available in February wherever Harlequin Books are sold.   VAL93

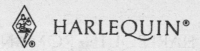 HARLEQUIN®

THE TAGGARTS OF TEXAS!

Harlequin's Ruth Jean Dale brings you
THE TAGGARTS OF TEXAS!

Those Taggart men—strong, sexy and hard to resist...

You've met Jesse James Taggart in FIREWORKS!
Harlequin Romance #3205 (July 1992)

And Trey Smith—he's THE RED-BLOODED YANKEE!
Harlequin Temptation #413 (October 1992)

Now meet Daniel Boone Taggart in SHOWDOWN!
Harlequin Romance #3242 (January 1993)

And finally the Taggarts who started it all—in LEGEND!
Harlequin Historical #168 (April 1993)

Read all the Taggart romances!
Meet all the Taggart men!

Available wherever Harlequin Books are sold.

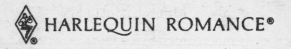

HARLEQUIN ROMANCE®

Norah Bloomfield's father is recovering from his heart attack, and her sisters are getting married. So Norah's feeling a bit unneeded these days, a bit left out....

Orchard Valley

And then a cantankerous "cowboy" called Rowdy Cassidy crashes into her life!

"The Orchard Valley trilogy features three delightful, spirited sisters and a trio of equally fascinating men. The stories are rich with the romance, warmth of heart and humor readers expect, and invariably receive, from Debbie Macomber."
—Linda Lael Mille

Don't miss the Orchard Valley trilogy by Debbie Macomber:

VALERIE   Harlequin Romance #3232 (November 1992)
STEPHANIE   Harlequin Romance #3239 (December 1992)
NORAH   Harlequin Romance #3244 (January 1993)

Look for the special cover flash on each book!

Available wherever Harlequin books are sold.   ORC-3